Ashley looked out at the congregation again, a sense of foreboding gripping her. Maybe the next exciting thing to happen at Primrose Hill would be the public humiliation of the pastor's wife.

Ashley Dennison's Former Lesbian Lover Visits Church. She could see the shock and horror on the faces of the saints as they digested that scandalous information in her mind's eye and it made her shudder with humiliation.

Regina's eyes connected with hers as if she knew what she was thinking. Ashley closed her eyes briefly and tried hard to focus on anything but her feeling of impending doom.

When she opened her eyes again and looked in the back row she saw that Regina was gone.

She breathed a sigh of relief but then she wondered, *Gone for how long?*

ON THE REBOUND 2

BRENDA BARRETT

JAMAICA TREASURES

On The Rebound 2

A Jamaica Treasures Book/October 2015

Published by Jamaica Treasures
Kingston, Jamaica

This is a work of fiction. Names, characters, places, and incidents are either the product of the author's imagination or are used fictitiously. Any resemblance to an actual person or persons, living or dead, events, or locales is entirely coincidental.

978-976-8247-34-6
Jamaica Treasures
P.O. Box 482
Kingston 19
Jamaica W.I.
www.fiwibooks.com

ALSO BY BRENDA BARRETT

FULL CIRCLE
NEW BEGINNINGS
THE PREACHER AND THE PROSTITUTE
AFTER THE END
THE EMPTY HAMMOCK
THE PULL OF FREEDOM
REBOUND SERIES
THREE RIVERS SERIES
NEW SONG SERIES
BANCROFT SERIES
MAGNOLIA SISTERS
SCARLETT SERIES

ABOUT THE AUTHOR

Books have always been a big part of life for Jamaican born Brenda Barrett, she reports that she gets withdrawal symptoms if she does not consume at least two books per week. That is all she can manage these days, as her days are filled with writing, a natural progression from her love of reading. Currently, Brenda has several novels on the market, she writes predominantly in the historical fiction, Christian fiction, comedy and romance genres.

Apart from writing fictional books, Brenda writes for her blogs blackhair101.com; where she gives hair care tips and fiwibooks.com, where she shares about her writing life.

You can connect with Brenda online at:
Brenda-Barrett.com
Twitter.com/AuthorWriterBB
Facebook.com/AuthorBrendaBarrett

Chapter One

Church.

She was in church.

Regina sat in the back of the picturesque neat building and looked around with a sense of disbelief. This is what Ashley had unknowingly driven her to, going to church just so that she could see her.

And not any old church either--this church was the epitome of conservativeness. It gave her the creeps. It reminded her of those long ago days when she stayed with her grandparents after her parents divorced. But even then her grandparent's church could not compare to this medieval looking edifice. Everything was minimalist and white, from the gleaming church floors to the material they had covering the podium. The only splash of color was a floral bouquet with some daffodils; their bright yellow blooms were some of the biggest that she had ever seen.

She admired them for a while and then continued to look

around in disbelief. The people coordinated with the Spartan decor. From what she could tell from her position in the back row, the women wore long dresses covering their knees...and hats! *Good lord, who still wore those kind of broad-brimmed hats in the twenty-first century...and blouses buttoned up to their neck?*

And if that was not bad enough, everybody had unprocessed hair except for a braid or two. No one had on makeup or jewelry that she could see.

Even Ashley, Miss Fashion Plate, sitting at the front of the church, was looking plain and unadorned, not even a ring on her finger.

At least she can bring off the plain look, Regina thought, admiring her for a while. Ashley did not need makeup or any of that stuff to look pretty. Her hair was natural now and the bun she had under the ridiculously frilly blue hat looked curly and thick.

Ashley looked softer somehow, younger if that were possible, and innocent...*no not innocent, pious...that was the word*. She hadn't seen Ashley in person for five years, ever since Ashley's divorce from Brandon Blake.

Regina had kept tabs on her though; even when she had gone to live in the UK and was working as a sports journalist she had hired an investigator to track Ashley.

His reports had been monotonous; Ashley did nothing really remarkable that first year after her divorce. The second year she had started going back to church in earnest and started this mad path she was on to recreate herself into this holy creature. The third year she visited her mother in the States for three months and they seemed to be getting along. The fourth year, Ashley met a guy, Ruel Dennison.

A pastor.

Of all the professions in the world? Regina had been

flabbergasted. Ashley really seemed to have a type. She liked straitlaced conservative Christian men. Brandon had been the epitome of straitlaced conservatism and she had thought that Ashley would not have stood a chance with him.

She was wrong then and she was wrong now because this pastor, Ruel Dennison, had married Ashley eleven months ago.

He was even more conservative than Brandon, if her reports from King, the investigator, were right. The pastor was forty years old, a widower with one child, a girl around sixteen, who still lived with her grandmother.

The pastor had met Ashley at one of those things that churches have—a convention. It was an event where church folks came together and stroked each other's egos, or that was how Regina imagined it, having never been to one.

As far as she knew Ashley had not told him about her and their past together and she was banking on the shock factor to get Ashley out of here and away from Ruel Dennison, minister of the gospel. Surely he wouldn't want a wife who had a past like Ashley's. That was her ace card. Ashley made it so easy with her choice of men.

It gave Regina power and she was not afraid to use this ammunition to once more break up Ashley's happily-ever-after with whatever sucker she had managed to lure into her web.

Regina truly believed that Ashley had gotten in over her head. *Surely she can't be enjoying this imprisonment in a small hick town in the back of beyond.*

It was possible that the pastor had worked some sort of voodoo on her or given her some sort of magic pill for her to be staying in this place. Surely it was not normal or natural to be this buttoned-up and suppressed. It boggled Regina's mind that Ashley, who had just turned thirty-five, could enjoy this kind of hemmed-in lifestyle.

Regina had to rescue Ashley. She had to do something. Her two months' vacation before she joined a local television station as head of their sports department would have to be spent up here in Hicksville trying to get Ashley to see sense once again. And this time she was sure that Ashley would listen.

She looked around the church. It had two pews, it could comfortably seat sixty persons and the front benches were relatively full. She had come at the right time, it seemed. Somebody was reading a scripture passage and the rest of the audience was following from their Bibles...*no, not audience, congregation.*

They called the gathering of a people in a church congregation. She was going to have to brush up on her church vocabulary.

She hunkered down in her seat even further. She stuck out like a sore thumb. She had recently pierced her eyebrow and the tattoo of the bird that she had gotten just last month in a drunken dare with one of her friends was in livid relief against her neck. Not to mention that she was in a ruby red sleeveless pantsuit. Her arms were showing! Bring on the church police. She looked around. *Did they have church police?*

She tried not to chuckle at her silliness as someone announced prayer. The congregation in unison pulled out kneeling pads from the pockets in the church benches and knelt.

She followed—why not? She hadn't knelt in years and though her new Versace pants were perilously close to the ground, she still knelt. She didn't want to stick out even further. Fortunately, the place was tiled in what looked like white marble.

The church was so quiet you could hear the trees rustling near the building as they swayed in the wind. *This is probably what is meant by reverence,* she thought. It was nice, soothing. She could get used to this part of the church thing.

No noise. Just silence. And then the lady who was supposed to pray started, shattering the silence with her heavy, almost manly voice.

"Good Lord, we are sinners; deliver us from our sins…"

And then she went on and on, like she was preaching, and the rest of the once-docile congregation started shouting amen intermittently. It was crazy.

Regina cracked one eye open and then the other. Was this the sermon? Why did she have to shout?

"You are a visitor," a pleasant-faced lady whispered and knelt beside her in the middle of the marathon prayer.

"Yes," Regina whispered back. "Is it so obvious?"

The lady quirked her brow at Regina and then smiled. "Yes."

She closed her eyes and bowed her head like everybody else and Regina looked at her curiously. Middle aged, obviously as conservative as the rest of the people here. Her hair was peppered with gray and she was in one of those broad-brimmed hats. She was plump and pleasant; she had actually smiled with her—a far cry from the reception that she thought that she would get from these country folks stuck in the seventeen hundreds.

Regina was under no illusion that she looked anything near conventional; she even got funny looks from non-Christian people, even though she had her Mohawk style dyed in a more conventional orange-red color these days. Her eyebrow, nose and tongue piercings were a bit much for the more traditional public, as her mother would take pains to point out to her time and time again.

When the prayer was over they got up. The lady looked at Regina. "I am Lynette Skinner. You can call me Lyn."

"Hey." Regina nodded. "I am Regina Tharwick. You can call me Regina."

Lyn grinned. "You are from Kingston or some foreign place, huh? I can tell from your accent."

"Yes." Regina didn't elaborate; she liked to think that she didn't speak with any accent but she definitely didn't sound like anyone from Primrose Hill. She figured that Lyn Skinner was being kind.

Lyn moved in closer to her. "I am just returning to church after being banned. I am not really qualified for the front benches. So I guess I will stay around here with you. They treat me like a stranger anyway…the bunch of hypocrites."

"What did you do?" Regina asked curiously. She felt warmed by the fact that Lyn was not only not judging her but was speaking to her as if they were friends.

Lynette frowned and then looked around. There was no one else up to three benches before them and only the windows to the right. There was nobody to overhear them if she whispered.

"I was disfellowshipped." Lynette leaned in closer to Regina.

"What's that?" Regina was looking at Lynette, fascinated now. "Is that like being expelled from school?"

"Something like that, but more like a suspension." Lynette crossed her hands primly over her lap. "I am still not a full member again yet. They have me on probation. As if…" Lynette snorted.

"What did you do?" Regina's interest was piqued now. She didn't know that churches suspended people for wrongdoing, but it made sense. They were an institution just like school.

And if they had a dress code and stuff, it stood to reason that there would be punishment.

"My employees, the Kincaids... Them." Lynette pointed her thumb in the direction of a couple who were sitting near the front. They looked to be in their late forties or early fifties. It was hard to tell from the distance. The man had his hand around his wife in easy familiarity. The lady was in a heavy embroidered dress with long sleeves. It looked expensive but completely out of place in the hot June weather and in this neighborhood, where everybody else seemed to dress simply.

She also had a matching embroidered hat that was so wide at the rim that Regina couldn't see her face.

"What did you do?" She focused her attention back to Lynette.

"Nothing to be disfellowshipped about," Lynette whispered. "They have a farm, a big farm, and I just took a bag of oranges without their permission. Granted, it was a big bag and I had all intentions of selling it but still... They were not around for me to ask. The wife was in the States on business and the husband was out for the day, God knows where.

They have a half-mad son, him," she indicated a young man who was crouched around the keyboard near the platform area.

He was thin, very thin, and very light-skinned, almost albino like. He wasn't albino though. He looked up as if sensing Regina's gaze and his eyes connected with hers briefly before he looked down again. There was a young girl preparing to sing and he played the first notes from the song.

"He doesn't look mad," Regina whispered, finding that she was enjoying herself immensely since Lyn showed up.

"Well, he's not really mad. His brain is messed up from

smoking marijuana or something like that." Lyn snorted. "Let's just say that he comes and goes. You know..."

"Lucid and crazy at the same time." Regina nodded. "Got it."

"Well, he caught me with the oranges and created such a ruckus, next thing I know they were calling me a thief, almost turned me into the police, and then the wife suggested that they should handle it at the church level. If you saw the way she was haughty about saying it, too…

"They carried me to the church board and condemned me like I was some horrible thief who deserved to be hanged. God sees and knows that I am no thief.

"I worked for them for twenty years and I never took a thing. Taking a bag of oranges when they have hundreds if not thousands of oranges dropping off the tree--is that a sin?"

"That's so unchristian," Regina murmured, egging on Lynette, who looked like she was on the verge of frothing at the mouth.

"Yes," Lynette harrumphed, "they should be the ones disfellowshipped for meanness to me. The man, Mr. Owen Kincaid," Lynette whispered, leaning even closer to Regina, "is an elder in this church. He sits on the church board and makes all of these decisions, and I know for sure that he is not holy. You should see the kind of things that are on his computer."

Regina whispered. "Like what?"

"Stuff. Really disturbing stuff," Lynette said, changing the subject quickly realizing that she had said too much. "The woman, Norma Kincaid, is the queen bee of the hills. She acts like she is the closest person to heaven but listen, she is not holy either. Something is off about her. I may not be able to pinpoint what it is but let me tell you, something is definitely fishy.

Lynette smiled. "She appointed herself as choir director and she can't sing and nobody has the guts to tell her that her key is not on any musical register. The women around here, even the pastor's wife, hang on to every word she says as if she is God. She acts as if Norma is the first lady, not the other way around. That in itself is wrong, isn't it?"

"Very wrong," Regina said solemnly.

"They are the richest people around here though, and they do help out a lot of the families. I have to give that to them. You know Ashford Manor?"

"Nope." Regina shook her head. She had just driven through miles of greenery and no civilization up to the hill where the church was perched. Everything had looked like one blur of rural greenery. She couldn't remember seeing any house.

"They own Ashford Manor." Lynette snorted. "Who calls their house manor? Ridiculous if you ask me, and it is just a plain old house. Maybe because they own nearly all the land up here. They think that they are some kind of royalty. And to think a couple of years ago they were not even that wealthy."

"Really?" Regina's interest was more than piqued now.

"Don't ask me how they went from ordinary to much." Lynette huffed. "I am not one to gossip...but let me tell you, the Kincaids are not saints."

"Not saints," Regina repeated.

"Them...the Allens are not saints either," she stabbed her hand in the direction of an Indian lady in the front, who was fanning herself with what looked like an old-time hand fan that folded to look like a stick but opened up like an accordion.

"She is a nurse at the community center, and the one that just prayed sits on the church board too," Lynette said harshly.

"Nurse Honey Allen is not worthy to judge me either. I think people listen to her because she has all of that long, dark hair. I don't think she is even pretty."

"Ooh, that was catty." Regina glanced at Lynette. "But I agree, she is not that pretty."

"Him," Lynette pointed her nose to a gentleman who was sitting closer to them, three rows up. "He acts like he is the moral police: everything is wrong, nothing is acceptable, everybody should eat vegetarian and buy his vegetables. You should have seen how the old Pharisee thrummed his nose up at me in the meeting. He called me a thief."

"Who is he?" Regina whispered. So her thoughts were not that far off; they really did have a church police!

"Conroy Coke. He owns a popular aquaponics farm up here. He sells his fish but constantly talks about being vegetarian, the hypocrite. He sits on the board too. That guy over there is his son."

She pointed over the aisle toward a young guy probably in his twenties, very good-looking in a smooth, slim-faced kind of way.

"He is not nearly as bad as his Pharisee father. He actually asked for mercy for me but it is so obvious that he lusts after the pastor's wife that I couldn't help but think that he is just looking for company in his sinful ways."

She folded her arms. "Then again, he recently returned to Primrose Hill under mysterious conditions. Maybe he had other sinful things going on in his life."

"Mmm," Regina murmured. "Mysterious huh? Where was he?"

"Kingston," Lynette said without hesitation. "He had a big accounting job with a company there. He just showed up here last year and they gave him a church post just like that. He is now the treasurer. And I have been in this church for years...years! Did they give me that post? Oh no! They gave it to him."

"Really terrible." Regina bit her lip and suppressed the smile that was on the verge of breaking out on her face. Lyn Skinner was something else, and she couldn't remember ever enjoying church half as much as she was enjoying it now.

"What's his name?" She was interested in this mysterious guy, who was now the church treasurer and had a crush on Ashley.

An idea was forming in her head thanks to Lynette. The more Lynette kept pointing out the offenders of holiness, the more she thought how easy it would be to convince Ashley to leave this place. It would be one more thing to use in her arsenal.

If Ashley could see that these people were not good for her, maybe she would want to come back to Kingston and forget this self-imposed Christianity nonsense.

"Josiah Coke." Lynette glanced at her, breaking her chain of thought. "You know him?"

"No." Regina shook her head. "Kingston is a pretty big place and I am just passing through here, really. Never seen him before."

Lynette looked as if she didn't believe her. And why should she? Primrose Hill was not a place you just passed through. It being in the hills, there was nowhere else to go. It was off the beaten path.

"It is quiet up here." Regina was forced to defend herself at Lynette's skeptical gaze. "Sometimes a person just needs to escape."

Lynette accepted her excuse without comment. "Can you believe that they gave Josiah Coke the treasurer post? They don't even know if he's a thief or anything."

Regina smiled; the irony of Lynette being concerned that

this guy Josiah was a thief was not lost on her. She said out loud, "It seems like these folks are not as medieval and boring as I thought."

"Boring no. Medieval yes." Lynette grunted. "I am sure that even the pastor and the first lady have interesting lives. They are people, you know. Everybody has something to hide, except me." Lynette shrugged. "I didn't hide the fact that I was taking the oranges to sell. I didn't lie but all of these secret keepers condemned me for it."

She breathed out after that last statement and then leaned back in her chair, a scowl on her face.

Regina's ears perked up after her last statement. *The pastor? Ashley's holy husband.* Why hadn't she thought to look into him before?

Maybe because she had found only good things when she had investigated Brandon, Ashley's first husband, a couple of years ago. She didn't want to waste her time with this minister of the gospel.

He should be even squeakier clean than Brandon. The thought was nauseating for her. Squeaky clean was so...so boring.

"Where are you staying?" Lynette leaned forward again.

Regina shrugged. She had not thought that far ahead. She didn't know if she could stay an hour more in the country much less a day.

"My aunt is renting out her house for the next couple of years," Lynette continued, "short term rentals only, though. Fully furnished and you have maid service, me."

She pointed to herself and grinned. "I don't have a job now so you'll get the best cleaning service available and I cook too, I cook really well. Maybe that's what I am going to do now that I am jobless. Cook and sell to school children."

"I'll think about it," Regina whispered to her.

"If you want peace and quiet up here is the place for it."
Lynette put on her most persuasive voice.

Regina nodded and then focused on the front of the church
again. During the whispered conversation with Lynette the
young lady had screeched out a song and was now finished
singing.

Ashley got up to speak. She was in a demure pale blue
skirt suit that highlighted how trim and in shape she was.
She was smiling when she started speaking. Even from the
back Regina could see the happiness on her face.

"Brothers and Sisters, today the speaker is none other than
our beloved pastor, Pastor Ruel Dennison, a man of God, a
truly good husband and provider. I ask for your undivided
attention as he puts God's word before you."

The church people said Amen.

Ashley glanced toward the back before taking her seat and
her eyes widened.

Regina gleefully observed that she stumbled. Ashley had a
dazed expression on her face as she took her seat. She closed
her eyes and again looked at the back row where Regina was
sitting.

A look of horror crossed her face and Regina could see her
swallowing in what looked like panic—or was it fear?

She couldn't resist giving a brief hello wave to Ashley, and
then blew her a kiss.

Ashley closed her eyes again and Regina saw that even
when her husband started speaking, she didn't open them.

You can't shut me out, Ashley. She looked at Ashley,
knowing that a wide smile was on her face. *No way, I am
back and you are coming back to Kingston with me.*

She made a mental note to call King; she needed a dossier
on everyone on this church board, including the pastor. Lyn
might be a disgruntled church sister caught in the midst

of stealing but she had just whetted Regina's appetite to investigate this church board.

It was good to come armed with information when she approached Ashley in the not–too-distant future. And maybe, just maybe, it would be worth a stay here in this place if the findings proved to be interesting enough.

Chapter Two

No. Ashley heard a ringing in her ears as she sat down. *No. No. No. Not Regina.*

Her heart was pounding hard in her chest, as if it wanted to escape the confines of her body.

She had closed her eyes in fear because surely she was hallucinating. When she opened them and looked around the platform where her husband had stood up to speak she saw that Regina was still there.

She closed her eyes and looked again. Yes, she was still there, a knowing smirk on her face, a typical Regina expression. A shaft of sunlight illuminated her as if she was on a stage and most of her upper arm tattoos and her piercings were highlighted in sharp relief.

Ruel was bound to see her. Ashley closed her eyes again. She had only just gotten around to telling him about Regina.

He had taken the other things she had done in stride, her marriage her divorce, the deception with Brandon. He had moved past that and asked her to marry him anyway. She had been reluctant to tell him about her time with Regina but in the spirit of absolute transparency that they had between them she couldn't hide it anymore and she had only just told him last week.

Surprisingly, he hadn't been as understanding about that time in her life as she thought he would be. He had been fine about adultery, he had understood about her less than motherly ways but he had actually looked angry and spoken to her harshly after her hasty confession about Regina.

That was very unlike him. Ruel was the epitome of gentleness and understanding; she could tell him anything.

Ashley wondered now if he sometimes wished he hadn't married her and gotten exposed to the sordid life she had lived. He was in many ways an idealist, and innocent. She had way more experience about life than he did.

At forty he hadn't veered off the straight and narrow much. He had gotten married to Rosalie Miller right after college. They had a child together, a daughter they named Jorja.

They had even gone on missionary work together all over the globe. They were the ideal Christian family. To hear Ruel tell it, they had been perfect, two peas in one harmonious pod until Rosalie died in a car accident a year and one month ago while they were on vacation in the States.

Ashley got married to Ruel two months after Rosalie's death; it was far too close to his first wife's death in her opinion but Ruel had insisted that he loved her, warts and all. Loved her enough not to wait through a reasonable grieving period.

Had Ashley known that he was a recent widower she would have waited. As it was, she still had a niggling doubt that they had gotten married too soon and that she was the rebound wife.

Ruel did not know what he was getting himself into; she was no Rosalie. But Ashley had sworn to God that in her next relationship she was going to come clean and tell all. She had not spared Ruel any details as to exactly what she was to Regina and what they used to do.

And now...he was only just getting around to digesting that piece of information about her when Regina popped into her life once more. Regina always showed up in her life like a bad penny to cause havoc and trouble.

She gritted her teeth angrily and tried to concentrate on the sermon but she felt a sense of injustice so strong she had to clamp her hands on the chair not to get up and walk down the short aisle of the church, reach for Regina and shake her and shout, "Why can't you just leave me alone? I have moved on! I have changed. I am not the Ashley you knew! You parasitic, evil beast!"

Her husband's voice penetrated her feverish thoughts. He was passionately preaching about doing the will of God.

"Sin has its consequences," he said in his smooth voice. "Some consequences are immediate; some take a while to work themselves out. Look at David. After his little stunt with Uriah's wife, the baby they had died and the prophet said that the sword would never depart from his house. Even if you ask for forgiveness, some things will come back to haunt you. The safest thing to do is to not sin in the first place. Fortunately, God is merciful, but we must not forget that he is also a judge and he will bring every deed into judgment with every secret thing, whether it be good or evil...great or small."

He was going to be doing one of his hard messages today. She tensed herself for it. She usually enjoyed his preaching but now she feared that this sermon would hit closer to home than usual.

Regina was here.

Her past transgression was sitting in church with a smirk on her face. This did not bode well for her. She could feel it. After five years of relative peace and safety, her greatest mistake was back.

Regina worried her. She was not known to keep her tongue. The effect that her evil tongue could have on Ruel's ministry could be catastrophic.

Primrose Hill was where he partially grew up; like so many young people he had left the place to find greener pastures. After Rosalie's death he had asked to be assigned here and the higher-ups in the church had obliged him.

When she had moved to Primrose Hill after marrying Ruel the people had accepted her at face value. They had been happy that their new pastor remarried and again found happiness.

Primrose Hill people were old school, most of them farmers. The district was small, with a population of about two hundred and dwindling. The young people usually left as soon as they graduated high school. The people of Primrose liked things the way they were, uncluttered and simple.

The most exciting thing to happen to the community in recent memory was the opening of the new community center by the Kincaids. Nothing much happened here and Primrose residents liked it that way.

Ashley looked out at the congregation again, a sense of foreboding gripping her. Maybe the next exciting thing to happen at Primrose Hill would be the public humiliation of the pastor's wife.

Ashley Dennison's Former Lesbian Lover Visits Church. She could see the shock and horror on the faces of the saints as they digested that scandalous information in her mind's eye and it made her shudder with humiliation.

Regina's eyes connected with hers as if she knew what she was thinking. Ashley closed her eyes briefly and tried hard to focus on anything but her feeling of impending doom.

When she opened her eyes again and looked in the back row she saw that Regina was gone.

She breathed a sigh of relief but then she wondered, *Gone for how long?*

*****

The Kincaids invited Ashley and Ruel to lunch after church and they were in the car alone, heading farther into the hills where the Kincaids' house, Ashford Manor, was located.

Ruel was sweaty so he took off his jacket and hung it at the back of the car seat. He looked over at Ashley.

"You look a little off. What's wrong?"

"Nothing we can't wait until tomorrow to talk about." Ashley smiled at him reassuringly, though she was feeling far from the calm, collected person she was projecting.

"If you say so." Ruel turned on his Gaithers Homecoming CD and started to sing along to *Jerusalem.*

He had a lovely singing voice and Ashley looked over at him smiled. He was always in a good mood after a sermon. He had told her once that preaching was his calling; he couldn't imagine doing anything else.

"It was a good sermon," she said out loud. "I liked it."

He glanced over at her and smiled. His teeth looked extremely white against his dark skin.

He was handsome, no doubt about that. Tall, dark, with a narrow, straight face. When he was serious he looked refined, like a school teacher or something. When he smiled his whole face smiled. His deep brown, almost black eyes smiled too.

He had kindly eyes. It was the first thing she noticed about him a year and a half ago when they first met. That and the fact that he was good looking.

"What?" He raised his eyebrows after the song finished. "You haven't shifted your eyes from me since we left church."

"Just thinking about the first time I saw you." Ashley grinned. "You preached the sermon 'If The Son Has Made You Free'. And I sat there fanning myself and thinking good Lord, he is fine.

"What a lustful church sister." Ruel grinned. "The first time I saw you, I thought, Lord please let her be single. You were in the lunch line at the convention and I was about to turn away because no woman as fine as you would not be taken. Just then I heard a church sister declare, 'Sis Ashley, the singles' convention is next week. You are coming, right?' So I stalked you the whole day until I got a chance to say hi."

Ashley smiled wistfully. "And the rest was history. Who could have predicted that I would end up here, though?"

She looked outside the window at the farmlands on both sides of the road. She could remember her first visit to Primrose Hill. She had been shocked at the remoteness of the place and the fact that it was so rural. After the shock had worn off she begun to appreciate it.

The air was so clean and even though they were going through a drought it was relatively green. At this time of the year, the trees were heavy with fruit, especially mangos. She always thought that Primrose Hill should be called Mango Hill. There were so many variety of mangos. The air smelled heavily of the ripe fruit in the summer.

Besides the fact that Primrose Hill had its own kind of rustic charm, she would have gone wherever Ruel went. She realized that she had changed that much. She would follow wherever his ministry took him.

She hadn't even minded that she had to give up her precious clothing store. She had sold it without feeling a tinge of regret. The fresh country air, the true connection with a community, living for others and not just herself had been a welcome change to her usual routine and she liked it. She even liked her job as part-time business teacher at the high school.

Regina's face flashed before her and she grimaced. Regina's presence here was going to mean trouble. She could feel it but she didn't want to dwell on that right now. It was like having a perfect day and then watching as rain clouds form along the horizon.

The farmlands petered out into smaller lots and then houses appeared along the road. On this section of Primrose Hill the houses were newer and the gardens were pretty with their colorful bougainvillea plants climbing the fences.

Quite a few returning residents had come back to their community and built some large houses. Ashley and Ruel lived in one of them, a lovely five-bedroom house which was too large for just the two of them but was willed to Ruel by an uncle who had intended it for his retirement home but had died before getting the chance to even see it.

They passed Honey Allen's house. She had the prettiest yard in the neighborhood. Even in drought conditions her lawn was almost electric green and her flowers were healthy and blooming. The daffodils and African daisies were blooming side by side in a riot of colors.

Ruel slowed down without her asking so that she could enjoy the view.

"Gorgeous," Ruel murmured. "Honey has a serious green thumb. It is a gift, really. I think so."

"And Oliver to help her and the water from Conroy's

fish farm," Ashley murmured, straining her neck to see the garden. She was almost feeling sorry that they had passed the visual beauty of Honey Allen's yard.

A few houses later, they passed their house, which was really unremarkable from the road. The lawn looked more brown than green and even their bougainvillea trees looked scraggly. Honey's yard put hers to shame, by far.

The Kincaids' giant mansion was at the end of the road. There were no other houses after that, just a grove or two of mango trees and acres of orange trees which were slowly dying because of a citrus disease.

Owen and Norma always had a crowd over for lunch after church. They were a wealthy couple and quite generous with it.

Ruel drove up to the house, which didn't look like much in terms of architecture. It was just a sprawling square white building but nobody who came up here thought about the architecture of the house.

Ashley got out of the car and looked out over the almost three hundred and sixty degree view of farmlands and rivers sparkling in the distance.

Ruel laughed when he saw her thunderstruck expression. "The view never gets old, does it?"

"No." Ashley shook her head. "Seriously, it doesn't and I have been here for close to eleven months now. Maybe in another year or so I will be just as blasé about it as you all seem to be."

Ruel pulled her closer to him and pointed to a sliver of water far off in the distance. "That is Milk River Bath."

"I can barely see it." Ashley laughed. "I thought Owen had said it was that way." She spun around and pointed in the opposite direction.

"Owen has always had directional problems," Ruel said

jokingly. "I say it is that way."

"Ah, Pastor Ruel," Owen came from his vehicle grinning. "That same old geography debate again."

He helped Norma out of the car and she came out smiling.

Ashley admired them. They were a handsome couple. Owen was tall and big. Not muscular, just large. He was fighting a losing battle with a paunch. He had level eyebrows which looked like they always needed a trimming, a hawkish nose, and a mouth that was always on the verge of smiling.

They called him the gentle giant at church. Whenever they did a reenactment of David and Goliath he would play the part of the giant. But no one took him seriously. He wasn't a scary enough Goliath, especially when he wriggled those bushy eyebrows.

Norma was tall, too, and slim. Her figure hadn't gone the way of Owen's. At first glance Norma looked cold and haughty.

Maybe it was her aquiline nose and her plucked eyebrows which gave her the expression of haughtiness and the fact that she always wore her hair in a tight chignon that highlighting her cheekbones. She made no attempt to soften her features.

She looked like a disapproving headmistress ninety percent of the time, but she was really a very nice person.

Owen and Norma were the first to welcome Ashley when she arrived in the district eleven months ago. Norma had been especially warm and whatever Norma did, the rest of the church sisters followed meekly.

Norma Kincaid had more influence than anyone at Primrose Hill. People deferred to her without even realizing it, and that included her, Ashley admitted to herself. She had found herself like everyone else, just accepting that Norma knew best.

Norma was not the typical genteel country lady. She

spent quite a bit of time overseas and she was effortlessly sophisticated. Ashley knew when someone was faking sophistication and this lady was not. Even now, standing beside Owen in her intricately embroidered dress, she oozed class.

She removed her hat and came over and hugged them, her smile genuine and friendly. Her face was a cool honey brown and unlined. Owen boasted that she had been the town beauty back in the day. Ashley could well believe him, especially when she smiled.

They were both in their early fifties—not over the hill yet by any means.

"Ruel, you should give it up," Norma laughed. "Even though you grew up here, you did leave as a teenager. Clarendon geography is Owen's specialty."

Ruel laughed good-naturedly. "Okay then. I give up."

"Come on in." Norma hooked her hand in Ashley's. They were almost the same height, "I invited the board members and their families today. I thought the new junior pastor would have been here, Ruel. I thought that now would have been a good time to break bread with us."

"He had another appointment." Ruel walked beside Owen. "He should be here next week."

"Good." Norma opened the door and they trooped behind her into a tastefully decorated living room, which took advantage of the view with sliding glass doors. A steady cool breeze was wafting through the doors and Ashley made a beeline for the door and the view.

Norma chuckled. "I am just going to ensure that Jilly has everything ready in the kitchen."

"Okay," Ashley said, relieved. She had been on the verge of offering to help when what she really wanted to do was go outside and take in the view.

Honey Allen was already on the veranda with her son Oliver. She was sprawled out on a lounge chair and looking contented.

"Sister Ashley!" She waved from her end of the veranda. "We got here before Owen and Norma. Jilly let us in."

Ashley smiled and walked over to them. Oliver was hanging at the balustrade and looking over pensively, as if he had a lot on his mind. He gave her a shy smile.

He was seventeen and in her business class at high school. His mother had insisted that along with the sciences he should take business classes.

Ashley smiled back at him. It was impossible not to smile with Oliver. He was a quiet boy and really beautiful to look at. He was Honey's only child and her most precious possession.

His father lived in Barbados, or so Honey said. Ashley had long suspected that Honey and her husband were estranged but Honey was living in denial. She sometimes made reference to her husband as if they were still communicating but Ashley didn't quite believe her. Mostly because when she mentioned him everybody around her went quiet. She would love to know what the story was but she was not willing to do any sort of heart to heart with Honey.

Honey was also curious about her. So there. They would not be having any heart to heart conversations anytime soon.

"Nice prayer today," Ashley said, settling down in a lounge chair beside honey. "I was blessed."

"Thank you." Honey nodded. "To God be the glory. My voice is rather husky, though. I think I must have damaged it while cheering for Oliver at sports day. He came first in the 100 meters and 400 meters races."

Ashley smiled. "Congrats, Oliver."

Oliver nodded. "Thank you Sister Ashley, though I would

prefer if Mommy stopped talking about it."

Honey smirked. "Never. You won, you should be ecstatic. This just proves that you can do anything. You can be a medical doctor as well as have an athletic career if you choose to."

Oliver rolled his eyes at his mother. "I had no competition; of course I was going to win. I am going to find Jack and hang with him."

"No," Honey said sternly. "What did I tell you about hanging around with Jack?"

"You said that he is a no-good, drugged-up disgrace for a human being."

"That's right," Honey said and then looked at Ashley sheepishly. "I also added that his only redeeming grace was his wonderful parents and the fact that he could play the piano."

Ashley didn't respond and Oliver shrugged and turned back to the view disinterestedly.

Jack Kincaid was the only son for Norma and Owen. They had two older girls who lived abroad, one in Japan and the other in Australia. They had fancy job titles that Ashley couldn't remember.

Jack was an anomaly in their perfect family. Apparently he had smoked marijuana when he was in his teens and it had affected his brain somehow. She hadn't stopped to find out how that happened, but she had always suspected that he had developmental problems and was just challenged that way. No one wanted to say that out loud though.

Most of the time Jack walked around like he was not aware of what was going on. And yet he always came to church with his parents and he played the piano beautifully. He was the church's official pianist.

Jack came out on the veranda and sat on the opposite

end of the veranda and ignored them. He usually didn't say much. Ashley could barely remember hearing him speak and she was in the district now for eleven months.

"So how are you settling into the school?" Honey asked, dragging her mind from Jack.

"Good. Thanks for asking." Ashley glanced at Oliver. "I didn't know that I would enjoy teaching in a million years but my short semester was good. Not surprising though, I have students like Oliver that make it worthwhile."

Honey nodded. "I like to hear that. Some girls came by the clinic the other day and the topic of conversation was you. Mrs. Dennison is so pretty, Mrs. Dennison talks so nice, Mrs. Dennison, this Mrs. Dennison that. You have a fan club."

Ashley laughed. "I guess I should be grateful that I am making some kind of impact."

Honey took the pins out of her hair one by one and her wavy, jet-black Indian hair fell almost to her waist. Not a grey hair in sight and she was what...forty-two or forty-three? Her skin was also glowing healthily. She was the head nurse at the health clinic and she was a good advertisement for them.

"So when are your two girls coming back to visit?" Honey asked casually. "What were their names again?"

"Alisha and Ariel." Ashley didn't want to talk about them to an obviously curious Honey.

Brandon had carried them to church six months ago to her welcoming ceremony and she and Ruel had not given any explanation for their existence. The curiosity must be eating up Honey; this was the third or fourth time she was inserting the girls into her conversation.

"Shouldn't we be helping Norma prepare lunch?" Ashley asked before Honey could question her more. She knew where the inevitable questions would lead. Honey wanted to know more about her ex-husband, her life before Ruel.

"Nah. She has it under control. Her new helper, Jilly, is here."

Ashley sighed.

"Your ex-husband is a really good looking man." Honey started fishing again.

"Hey," Conroy Coke came on the verandah, a broad smile on his face.

Ashley could not remember a time when Conroy's usually stiff presence was so welcomed.

He approached them, his face wreathed in smiles. "I passed pastor Ruel and Owen in the living room vigorously debating whether Daniel in the Bible was a eunuch."

Ashley laughed in relief. "So you escaped?"

"There is no room for me in that discussion." Conroy pulled up a chair and sat down. "I am not as intellectual as they are."

"Where's Josiah?" Honey asked, smiling with Conroy, completely forgetting that she had been questioning Ashley.

"He is outside on the phone," Conroy said lazily. "He'll be in soon."

"I'll go join him." Oliver shifted from the balcony.

"No." Honey held up her hand. "What's the matter with you? The man is on a phone call," Honey chastised Oliver.

"Why can't young people stay still?" She looked at Conroy, a small smile on her face.

Conroy responded by looking at Honey with unabashed adoration in his eyes.

Ashley watched them keenly. She had heard the story several times before about Honey and Conroy secretly seeing each other when they were younger. But Honey's parents did not approve since Conroy was a good six years older than their daughter.

They both left Primrose Hill years ago. Honey went to nursing school and Conroy to the police academy. They eventually married different people. Honey's husband now lived abroad and Conroy's wife divorced him.

Conroy had left the police force to return to Primrose Hill and to farming but he still had that stern police air about him except when he was around Honey. When the two of them were in the same room there was always a little tension and Conroy got all soft-looking and acted shy, like one of her pimple-faced high school students.

Ashley watched as Conroy dragged his eyes from Honey and settled in his chair. He had a similar view from his farm on the other side of the hill but he still seemed appreciative of this one. His face looked a lot more lived-in than Honey's, even though he was just a few years older.

Ashley had always thought that he looked a little like the boxer Mike Tyson without the tattoo. Same stocky build and same shaped face.

"We need some rain," Conroy said, clasping his hands across his chest.

"Tell me about it," Ashley said. "You know, I thought I saw rain clouds on the horizon today."

"But now they are gone." Josiah strolled onto the verandah. "When it actually rains we are going to have a flood. The ground is so dry it is cracking."

"Dooms-dayer," Conroy said to his son fondly. "How is your mother?"

"Fine." Josiah shrugged. "She is thinking of coming out to Jamaica next month."

Conroy grunted.

"Don't worry, she said she wasn't coming in your vicinity. You know who I saw today?" Josiah asked, changing the topic. "Lynne Skinner. She is back at church; isn't that something? Told you guys she'd be back."

Everybody straightened up, even Jack Kincaid, who had been ignoring them so far.

Lynne was a hotbed topic, especially at the Kincaid house. According to Norma, she had been steadily stealing from the family over the twenty years that she worked for them.

Josiah continued without even missing a beat; he obviously didn't care that Lynne Skinner was not supposed to be mentioned.

"And she was talking to Regina Carter."

"You mean that creature with the tattoos and piercings?" Honey shivered dramatically. "I hate tattoos. Piercings I am okay with, but not the way she has them. Good Lord."

"You hate everything hip or cool." Oliver turned around and became interested in the conversation.

Ashley stiffened. Josiah knew Regina?

"How do you know that creature?" Honey beat her to the question.

Josiah pulled up a chair and sat beside his father. "She used to play for the Jamaican football team. The girls' team. She was hands-down the best goalkeeper ever."

Ashley subsided in her chair, releasing the pent-up breath she was holding. She had forgotten about that part of Regina's history.

"I love football so much I even follow the girls' team," Josiah said. "Back in Kingston I used to go to every match. I wonder why Regina is up here though, and at church? She is not exactly the church type."

"A girl who plays ball." Oliver's eyes widened. "That's cool. I've never met a baller girl before."

Honey snorted. "And God forbid that you should. She must be a lesbian, this baller girl."

Ashley stiffened anew. For once Honey's snarky little

judgmental observations had hit the nail on the head.

"Mom, come on, because a girl plays ball doesn't make her a lesbian, just like a guy who wants to do nursing doesn't make him gay. Men and women do things that overlap the traditional roles."

Honey growled. "I don't care what you say, women are women and men are men. Full stop. Our grandparents had it right. Don't get me started on this topic, Oliver. I am among polite company."

Oliver shrugged. "You are just as ancient with your views as your great-grandparents were."

"You watch when we get home." Honey pointed at her son threateningly. "I am going to straighten out your head before you go to university. I don't know where you get your liberal thought processes from. I have been trying to curb your free thinking since you were born. I have failed somewhere."

Ruel cleared his throat, putting an end to Honey's theatrics. "Dinner is ready. Norma said to come and get it while it's hot."

He glanced at Ashley and he wasn't pleased, she could tell. He was smiling for the group but Ashley could see that the smile wasn't in his eyes. He had heard what Josiah said about Regina.

Chapter Three

"We need to talk," Ruel said abruptly as soon as they were in the car after the lunch, which had turned into an extended Bible study that Norma had dominated as usual.

Nobody, not even Ruel, seemed to know their Bible like her. She even knew whole chapters from memory. Ruel opened the door for Ashley and she got into the car.

"I know what this is about." Ashley turned to him before he started the vehicle. "It's Regina. I didn't invite her up here, Ruel. I don't know what to do about her. She's a stalker; it's only a matter of time before she..."

Ruel sighed. "No, it's not about Regina."

"Oh." Ashley sighed. "Okay. You looked a bit grim back there."

Ruel started the car. "I mean, we'll talk about her if you want."

"No." Ashley shook her head. "I don't want to. Well, not until I see what her next move is. Maybe this was just a token stop to torment me."

"Fine." Ruel nodded. "I wanted us to talk about a more pressing matter, Jorja."

"Jorja. Your daughter Jorja?" Ashley asked. "What about her?"

"My mother can't handle her anymore." Ruel tightened his hand on the steering wheel. "According to her, Jorja has gotten to be a bit of a handful. She's sneaking out at night, to God knows where, and she has gotten involved with the wrong crowd."

Oh. Ashley watched with a heavy feeling in her stomach as he tried to formulate the next words. She knew what they were going to be and she tensed up in anticipation of them.

"She has to come live with us." Ruel glanced at Ashley's stricken face briefly and then back at the road. "I know we discussed taking our time with the whole motherhood issue."

"Yes," Ashley said weakly. "We did. I suck at it, you know."

"No you don't; Alisha and Ariel adore you." Ruel paused. "You must have done something right."

"Not me," Ashley swallowed. "Nadine and Brandon. My children are sweet and affectionate and loving because of their stepmother and father. For a couple of years I didn't even see them much and to my shame, I didn't even feel a pang of remorse."

"But Jorja is sixteen," Ruel said. "She is not a baby. All we'll need to do is guide her in the right path. She will have about two years with us before she goes to university; we can make a difference in her life."

Ashley grunted. "I am not sure about that 'we' bit."

"Come on, Ashley." Ruel slowed down the car to allow a herd of cows to pass. Their owner was behind them. He waved to Ruel and Ruel tooted his horn in response. "Come on Ash, you teach high school, you have some experience with teenagers."

"Yup, and that's how I know that teenagers are horrible creatures."

Ruel chuckled. "Were you a horrible creature as a teenager?"

"No, as a matter of fact I wasn't," Ashley said proudly. "I was a bookworm. I became a horrible creature after my teenage years. And that's why I don't blame them for being horrible at that age. I say get it over and done with then."

Ruel turned into their driveway and stopped the car. He turned toward her. "You can do this. The truth is I miss my daughter and I feel a huge helping of guilt for having her live with my mom for so long. I want her to be around me again. The poor thing lost her mother and then me at almost the same time."

"You saw her recently," Ashley said, "and she would come and stay with us this summer too. It's not like you've abandoned her altogether!"

"I know," Ruel sighed, "but two months of the year does not a father make."

Ashley nodded. "Okay, but for the record let it be known that Jorja does not like me. At the wedding she avoided me like the plague and any overtures of friendship were deliberately rebuffed."

"We'll get through that," Ruel said confidently. "You are such a wonderful person to live with. Jorja will see that. How could she not?"

Ruel picked up her hand and kissed it.

"When is she coming by?" Ashley asked, taking a deep breath. She was not as confident about Jorja liking her as Ruel was.

"In two weeks," Ruel said, "at the end of her exams, July 1."

*****

There are worse places I could spend my vacation. Regina looked around the cottage where she was going to spend her summer. She had stayed away from Primrose Hill for two weeks. She had only returned the place after getting some interesting preliminary reports from King. He had spent the last couple of days in the community gathering information, or so he said. She didn't know how he got his juicy information and she didn't care.

He was sitting across from her now with a stack of files on his lap, waiting for the balance of his pay, no doubt.

She couldn't wait to sink her teeth into his reports, but he was hanging on to them tightly. She rummaged in her bag and pulled out her purse.

He was chewing gum and he popped it occasionally. He crossed his leg and adopted his tough guy persona, which didn't fit him too well, Regina thought snidely. He looked like somebody's kindly grandfather.

"Cash only."

"I know." Regina cut her eyes at him. "I know your terms by now."

King shrugged. "I should have charged you extra. This group of people have quite a bit of stuff going on. Their lives are like a soap opera. All of them."

"All of them?" Regina raised her eyebrows.

"Pay me and find out." King rubbed his chin impatiently.

"Okay already." Regina counted out a couple thousand dollars and handed it to him.

He took the money and then handed her the stack of files.

And in an uncharacteristic show of emotion King said gruffly, "You be careful."

"Why?" Regina tapped her fingers on the file impatiently. She couldn't wait to get started. "These people are not dangerous. They live in the middle of nowhere. What on earth could they be up to that could warrant that warning?"

King snorted. "Everybody is dangerous once pushed too far, and I am not sure what you are going to do."

"I am not going to push anybody," Regina said airily, resting back in the settee.

"I've worked for your father for years. I respect him. He is a good lawyer and I am sure if he knew what you were up to he would give you this advice. Don't trust nobody. I would tell you to mind your own business but that bit of advice is already redundant. You are here now. Don't forget that curiosity killed the cat."

Regina rolled her eyes. "But satisfaction brought it back."

King chuckled. "Haven't heard that rejoinder for a while." He got up and headed to the front door. "So what are you going to do with the info?"

"Go to church." Regina followed him. "What else?"

"It's unusual for someone to go to church and have a detective check out the church board first."

Regina shrugged. "I have my reasons."

King looked at her closely and then shook his head. "I am going to take my own advice and mind my own business."

"Good." Regina nodded.

He opened the door and saw that Lynette Skinner was opening the gate with a bright smile on her face.

"I would be careful with this one too," King murmured before heading down the walkway.

"Bye," Regina called after him. "Thanks."

King waved, not bothering to look back at her. He got in

his car and drove away.

"Who's he?" Lynette asked, coming up the walkway. "Husband?"

"No." Regina shook her head. King looked old enough to be her father. He had a grandfatherly air about him which made the people around him feel comfortable enough to spill their guts. Lyn must need glasses.

"Sorry," Lyn said, watching Regina frown. "Your dad then?"

"No!" Regina walked into the house. It was a ranch style three-bedroom house that was set on a large lot of land with several mango and guinep trees at the back and several varieties of flowers at the front. The lawn was almost completely brown from the drought.

Lynette walked behind Regina. "Sorry for questioning you. It is none of my business."

"That's right," Regina said abruptly, heading for what looked like the largest bedroom. It had a queen-sized bed in the middle of the room with a mosquito mesh covering it.

"Am I going to have to contend with mosquitoes?" she asked, shuddering at the thought.

"No, no," Lynette said quickly, "all the windows have screens and the doors too. The occasional mosquito may come in but there is nothing to worry about."

"Where's the AC?" Regina asked, looking around.

Lynette pointed to the ceiling fan, which was directly over the bed. "Trust me, it gets very cool up here in the nights. You won't need AC."

"This is going to be some summer." Regina looked around the simply furnished room and sighed. There was a bed, two side tables with brass lamps. There was also a sofa that matched the lamps, and a built-in closet with a long mirror in the center and a writing desk with a drawer on one end. A key was in the drawer lock with a spare hanging from it. So the drawer could be locked. Good, that would come in handy for her files.

"Do you want to see the rest of the place?" Lyn asked eagerly.

"No, not yet," Regina said, heading for the en suite bathroom. She opened the door and was relieved to see that it was modern looking and done in the palest green shade.

"Do you want me to help you unpack?"

"No thanks," Regina said, heading for the hall. She was careful not to leave the files out, especially with the mega-curious Lynette watching her every move with eager-eyed anticipation.

"Okay then, I'll start preparing lunch. How does stewed chicken in lots of pepper and yam and bananas sound?"

"Like I died and came to rural heaven." Regina grinned. "That sounds good."

"And there are snacks in the cupboards. I got a whole case of peanut milk and lots of biscuits. It's part of our service here."

"Thanks Lynette." Regina threw over her shoulders. "I am allergic to peanuts and milk. I am more allergic to peanuts though, so none of that ever, at all."

"No problem," Lynette said. "I know all about food allergies. Remember, you can call me Lyn."

"Yes, I will do so." Regina scooped up her files. She was going to look through them as soon as she could and then she would formulate a plan.

*****

Regina slept fitfully in the early morning hours after running through King's detailed files. The more she read on each person the more she was looking forward to meeting them to see what they were really like at church.

Some of the information in the files was troubling and King had given his conclusions about some of the goings-on in the people's lives and she was inclined to believe him.

He was right, things in Primrose Hill were not as they seemed. Now she knew why King cautioned her to be careful. She had opened Pandora's box.

She got up groggily after hitting the snooze button on her alarm more than twice. She knew that Ashley ran through the hills for exercise every morning, according to King's report. Ashley had always been a gym junky. Regina should have known that she was still into her exercising.

Regina groaned and rubbed her leg. She hated morning exercise. It reminded her of her time in the football squad, where they would train for some insane hours to build stamina. She waited for her knee to stop its usual early morning spasms and then she stretched.

She hastily pulled on her walking outfit and went outside. It was light out though it was just five-thirty. It was surprisingly chilly too. She could see her breath in the morning air. The flowers in the front lawn were laden with dewdrops. It was pretty, she had to grudgingly admit, and she went back inside for her camera and looked once more at Ashley's regular walking route that King had drawn for her. She had to pass this house. Unless she went around to the steeper Mango Hill.

He had said that she walked alone and Regina was banking on that being so this morning.

She went back outside and snapped a picture of the foggy front lawn. When the sun made an appearance she would capture the dew on the flowers.

She walked through the gate and stretched, waiting for

Ashley.

"Hey, Regina Tharwick!"

She spun around, almost losing her balance. It was a man's voice; he had a hoodie covering his head and was in a dark blue tracksuit. He pushed his hand toward her and grinned.

"Hi, I am Josiah Coke."

"Huh?" Regina was taken aback. How did he know her?

Coincidentally his file was the very last one that she read. She knew all about his job in Kingston and why he was mysteriously back in Primrose Hill.

She looked suspiciously at his grinning face.

"Sorry. I am a fan," he said hastily, "from back in your football days."

"Oh." Regina smiled, "those days are long gone."

"I know," Josiah nodded. "The good old days."

"You are too young to be talking about good old anything," Regina laughed.

"I am not that young." Josiah grinned, flirting with her. "I am twenty-seven."

Regina winced. *Was he really flirting with me?*

"So you are here for vacation?" Josiah pushed his hands into his pockets and rocked back on his heels, obviously ready for a long conversation.

God, no! Regina exclaimed in her head but she turned to him and stretched. "You could call it that. It is good to get away from the rat race sometimes. And you, you live here?"

"Yes, for the time being." Josiah shrugged. "My father has a farm. It's a large operation. I help him out."

Regina nodded, trying to stop herself from looking disinterested. She knew all about Conroy Coke's farm and his hydro system and how he was the biggest supplier of vegetables this side of the island. Even in the drought he was doing extremely well. Maybe she knew too much. Besides, she wanted Josiah to disappear. She wanted to talk to Ashley alone, without an audience.

She glanced at her watch. It was six o'clock on the dot. "I don't want to keep you from your workout then." She nodded to Josiah.

He looked disappointed. "Okay." He prepared to head up the hill and then he turned back and looked at her.

"We have a Bible seminar at our church every night for the next three weeks. Why don't you come over tonight?"

Regina grimaced. Every night for three weeks? How time consuming! But then again, after reading the files last night maybe the people at the church really needed the studies, especially the Kincaids.

"Well, okay then," she said to Josiah, needing him to be on his way. "I'll be there."

"Cool." He grinned at her and waved, running up the hill with effortless ease. He was in good shape.

Regina looked at him enviously, Since her knee injury and the last couple of years of partying, she would be panting like crazy before she even took three steps.

She walked slowly down the hill, snapping pictures of the colorful bougainvilleas that were lining the walls of most of the houses on the stretch.

She was previewing one of her pictures on the digital camera when she heard Ashley's stricken squeal behind her.

"Regina!" She turned around slowly and smiled at her.

"Hi Ashley, you are a sight for sore eyes."

She watched as Ashley took in great gulps of air, her body held stiff with indignation.

"What on earth are you doing here?" Her voice trembled a bit and Regina's smile got wider.

"I am here to rescue you from this place." Regina watched as Ashley rubbed her clammy hands down the side of her tight-fitting tracksuit.

"I don't need rescuing. Leave me alone," Ashley said, pointing at her. "Just forget that you ever knew me. Give me a break. Please. I am begging you!"

Tears formed at the corners of her eyes and she stomped past Regina, her thick curls bouncing behind her neck.

"Ashley," Regina picked up speed and her knees protested. "You have to talk to me, at least."

"No. I am not interested in what you have to say. Just leave." Ashley walked even faster and Regina half-ran, half-walked to keep up.

A farmer was heading up the hill, a bunch of green bananas on his head; he had a cutlass over his shoulder and a dog loping beside him. He called to Ashley, and that slowed her down a bit, giving Regina time to catch up.

"Will you listen to me?" she panted when she was almost at Ashley's shoulder. "This place is crazy rural; what can you like about here?"

"I am here with my husband and that's good enough for me," Ashley said through gritted teeth. "Nobody can know about my past association with you. Got that?"

Regina chuckled. "Still playing hide and seek with your past?"

"No." Ashley sighed. "I tell my husband everything."

"Really!" Regina exclaimed. "That's lovely for you. Does he tell you everything?"

"What's that supposed to mean?" Ashley snarled.

Regina inched away from her. Ashley looked mad enough to do her some bodily harm.

"It means," Regina said slyly, "that everybody has secrets, even your saintly Ruel. Doesn't it strike you as odd that he jumped to marry you barely two months after his previous wife died? You would be surprised to know that some of your so-called secrets pale in comparison to what some of your church brethren are up to."

"What?" Ashley squinted at Regina. "What are you talking about?"

"I had them investigated. Not everyone obviously, just the really key ones, like your church matriarch, Norma Kincaid, and her husband, Owen. That nurse woman Honey Allen and the Cokes, Josiah and Conroy. And your husband—his secret was a shocker. I don't think this guy Ruel can even walk in Brandon's pristine shoes...Not that I liked Brandon but still. How could a pastor be worse than his parishioners? Wait, you do call them parishioners, don't you?"

Ashley glanced at Regina sharply. "Have you lost your mind? Shut up this minute. You are a liar and a destroyer! Everything you touch is destroyed."

"A destroyer," Regina snorted. "Please, that's not bad compared to some of the folks you have been rubbing shoulders with up here."

Ashley gave her one last furious look and started jogging.

"Ashley seriously, you are acting so childish." Regina started to walk faster to keep up with her. "We need to talk. You can't just ignore me."

Ashley jammed the earphones that she had dangling around her shoulders back in her ears and picked up speed. Regina tried to keep up with her but she was having difficulty drawing air into her lungs.

She stopped trying when they reached the flat part of the hill.

"I will be here all summer!" Regina shouted to her retreating back. "You can't avoid me! And let me tell you, if you don't leave this place with me I am exposing all secrets. And when I do you'll have to leave anyway!"

Chapter Four

Ashley ran up Mango Grove, the steepest hill in the district. It was her nemesis hill. She could only go halfway up normally but this morning her feet had wings. The sound of Regina's voice, *If you don't leave this place with me I am exposing all secrets*, gave her the fuel to run over the hill and home.

When she reached her veranda she collapsed on the front steps, spent. Her legs felt like jelly and she battled to draw air into her lungs.

She had a problem. It was foolish thinking that after not seeing Regina again for the past two weeks that she had somehow vanished, never to return. She had prayed about it and was silently rejoicing that she had gotten rid of her Regina problem, but she couldn't have been more wrong.

She sprawled on the floor of the veranda panting, her head whirring with thoughts of how to escape the fallout that she knew was coming with Regina's presence here. She was going to get it. She knew it. And now was the worst time to have to deal with Regina, especially because Jorja was going to be around. She had just resolved that she would be the best role model she could be to the girl, and now this.

Jorja had only just arrived last night and she was one unhappy girl. She had barely greeted Ashley, had run to hug her daddy and had collapsed into his arms and into an extended crying jag that had gotten on Ashley's last nerve. Ashley resolved that she needed to be patient; she needed to remember that the girl had lost her mother a few short months ago and was living in uncertain times right now.

She had extended an olive branch and offered to help Jorja unpack but she had gotten an intense look of hatred. So intense in fact that it had given her nightmares that night.

Jorja had with that one look declared outright war. It was not hard to see that the household was going to be a battlefield in the near future.

Ashley pulled in one shuddering breath to steady herself; she could not stand this drama right now. She would make a valiant effort to try to have a relationship with Jorja but if that failed she didn't know what she was going to do.

"That was a loud sigh," Ruel said behind her gently. "What's wrong?"

Ashley swung her head around to look at him. He was still in his robe and slippers, a cup of tea in his hand.

"Nothing. Everything." She struggled to a seating position and leaned her head on one of the posts. "You wouldn't believe who I just met on the hill."

Ruel yawned and came to sit beside her. "I can't imagine who at this time of the morning. Farmer Townsend?"

"I did see him," Ashley said hoarsely. "But I also saw Regina. She's back."

"Ah." Ruel stiffened. "How do you know this?"

"I saw her this morning." Ashley sighed. "Near where old Mrs. Skinner has her vacation rental home. So I figure that is where she is staying."

Ruel clutched his cup tighter and didn't say a word.

Ashley sighed in the silence.

"It is better not to have these kinds of situations, isn't it?" Ruel finally said, glancing at her. "It is better to live righteously and uprightly in the first place and things like this will not happen."

Ashley felt her lower lip trembling. "You are right. I had a past that I am not proud of, and yes, it is coming back to haunt me. You saying this is not helping. Regina will make it difficult for not just me, but your ministry as well."

Ruel sighed. "Sorry. I am sorry. I didn't mean to come across as judgmental."

"So what are we going to do?" Ashley asked helplessly.

"Tell me about her," Ruel said, leaning on the opposite post and looking at Ashley.

"Like what?" Ashley asked defensively. "I already told you. She is an evil troll who I mistakenly had a relationship with back when I was a younger, much worse version of myself."

"I mean who is she? Does she have family? What makes her tick? That kind of thing." Ruel sipped his tea. "It may give me some insight into understanding her and this obsession she has with you."

"Her name is Regina Tharwick," Ashley said, slumping even further on the post. "She is thirty-five years old, the only adopted child of Paul and Elizabeth Tharwick. Paul is a lawyer and Elizabeth a scientist. They couldn't have children so they adopted Regina when she was a baby. They divorced years ago. They both tried to make up for the separation and Regina was caught between two parents who wanted to please her more than they should, so they created a monster. Regina's real mother was a mental patient or something like that."

Ruel frowned. "Really?"

"Yes." Ashley nodded. "Regina found out in college that her biological mother was mentally unstable and it depressed her for days."

"I can understand that," Ruel said sympathetically. "At least she didn't grow up with her. It can be draining on a person."

Ashley grunted. "I am past the sympathy place for Regina."

"Could she have inherited her birth mother's mental instability?" Ruel asked, concerned.

"Not that I know of," Ashley shrugged, "unless you want to call an unhealthy fixation on me mentally unstable."

"So what does she do?" Ruel put down his mug beside him and clasped his hand.

"She did journalism in college, made the national senior football team...played with them for years. Five years ago she was working at her father's law firm. I don't know anything about her lately and I don't care to know."

Ruel nodded. "But she keeps coming back to you."

"Like a particularly bad virus," Ashley murmured, hitting her head against the post not very gently. It hurt to do it but it was also helping the pressure in her head, like a sweet kind of pain.

Ruel watched her helplessly. "Ash..."

"I wish...she'd just disappear," Ashley groaned, "from the face of the earth."

Ruel cleared his throat. "Ashley..."

"You have no idea what it is like, do you?" Ashley felt weak, helpless—tears clamoring to clog her throat. "When somebody stalks you and hounds you and makes your life a living hell...It will probably go on until I am old or die, or she dies. When that happens then I will be free. Now wouldn't that be something?"

"That would be something...that we shouldn't even contemplate." Ruel gave Ashley a sympathetic glance. "Would she be open to counseling? Or any other intervention strategies?"

Ashley laughed. She couldn't help it. "I think Regina probably needs an exorcism more than counseling. Have you ever done an exorcism? Drive the demons out of her."

"No," Ruel shook his head, "but I could try."

"I was kidding. Don't you dare act concerned for her. She will eat you alive." Ashley got up. "She is poison. Pure evil. You know what's funny. She claims that she investigated the church board and that you all have secrets, including you."

Ashley laughed. "This stinks of desperation on her part. I mean what sort of secrets could you have?"

Ruel grimaced. "I might have gone sixty in a fifty mile zone."

Ashley sighed. "It's ridiculous, this whole thing. What's even worse Regina is claiming that she will reveal all secrets if I don't come back to Kingston with her."

Ashley gave a harsh, bitter sound that was more distress than mirth and headed inside. "I am going to bathe and try to see if I can wash this morning's bad encounter from my body."

She missed the fact that Ruel had stiffened and that he deliberately put down his mug. It made a little click on the tiles of the verandah. She also missed the fact that his breathing had gotten shallow and rapid as he digested her last statement.

Nor did she see the fluttering of the curtains at the living room window where Jorja had been listening.

*****

"Where's my dad?" Jorja walked into the kitchen after twelve in the afternoon when Ashley, in a fit of domesticity, was baking tea cakes for the evening Bible study group. She had more than five dozen laid out on the island when Jorja stepped in.

"Good afternoon to you." Ashley forced herself to smile at Jorja. "Your father is conducting a funeral in the town. He wanted to tell you himself but you were sleeping. He'll be back by three."

"Oh." Jorja sat on one of the stools in the kitchen and cupped her chin.

"Are you hungry?" Ashley asked, looking at Jorja and trying not to do so in disapproval. She was still in her nightgown, a skimpy, frilly little thing that highlighted her slim legs and her slightly above-average bust area.

Jorja was a shapely girl. She had a cute, slightly round face, a small cute nose and bow-shaped red lips which were in stark contrast against her dark and smooth complexion. There was not a pimple on her velvety dark skin.

Ruel was going to have his work cut out with beating back the boys from his girl.

Jorja gave Ashley one of her baleful *I can't stand you* stares.

"What do you have for brunch, stepmother dear?" Jorja asked mockingly. "Poison?" Ashley raised her eyebrows in consternation. "Excuse me?"

Jorja sneered. "I heard you and my father talking this morning about your friend who you would like to have killed."

"What!" Ashley slammed down the rolling pin she was

holding. "You are not supposed to be eavesdropping on things you don't know and couldn't possibly understand. And I didn't say anything about having her killed."

"Yes, you did," Jorja said sullenly. "I heard you say that you wish that she'd just disappear from the face of the earth and that when she is dead you would be free. My dad had to chastise you for saying it "

"That was frustration speaking. I didn't mean it." Ashley felt her temperature rising as she stared into Jorja's hateful face.

"I know you feel the same way about me." Jorja looked at Ashley knowingly. "Don't even bother to deny it. Grandma said that you hated children and that's why I couldn't come and live with my Dad."

"I don't hate children!" Ashley gasped. "What on earth was Miss Miriam telling you?"

"The truth." Jorja narrowed her eyes and gave Ashley a suspicious look. "The evidence is there; your own kids don't live with you. You must be a really bad parent for them to be living with their father. I don't trust you."

"Okay, that's it." Ashley rubbed her temples. Flour was in her hair and she could literally feel her pressure rising. "So how do you want us to play this?"

"What?" Jorja was still in the same position, watching Ashley as if she was slightly afraid.

"This whole evil stepmother, defiant stepchild routine?" Ashley murmured, her voice losing energy. "Do you have any rules in mind?"

"No," Jorja murmured, giving up her combatant stance in the wake of Ashley's almost disinterested tone.

"I have some rules," Ashley said, turning to the sink and washing her hands.

"What rules?" Jorja asked cautiously.

"I have a stepmother too," Ashley said, "so this whole situation is not strange to me. She had rules and they worked for us."

Jorja wanted to know more but she bit her lip rather than show Ashley any interest. She had always been curious about her new stepmother. Her father had married her so soon after her mother died and then dumped her on her grandmother, so that it was hard to warm up to the woman who was by all indications the reason her dad abandoned her for close to a year.

Ashley took off her apron and then pulled a stool and sat in front of Jorja. She folded her arms almost demurely in her lap.

"Here is what my stepmother told me when she just moved in with me and my father. Are you listening?"

Jorja shrugged.

"Don't shrug at people. It shows a distinct lack of respect." Ashley brushed a speck of flour from her skirt.

"You are not my mother," Jorja hissed promptly. "You can't tell me anything!"

"That is actually rule number one." Ashley looked at Jorja. "I am not your mother and I don't want to be. I won't even try to be. You are probably too resentful for that to happen and I don't want to try to be your mother. I could try for friend, though. Please let that sink in.

"I love your father and I married him. I am very open to loving you too, because you are a part of him, but here's the thing. If you cannot respect me in my own home, you should know that I am no doormat. I give as good as I get. If you don't want to eat my food, fine, cook it yourself. You are old enough to do it, and no food is off limits to you here; this is not a prison. You take care of your own clothes. If you want help in figuring out the washing machine I am available; if not, ask your dad.

"Please let it be known, though, that untidiness will not be tolerated in the common areas." Ashley put on her stoniest piercing stare. "And we respect each other's property. Don't go snooping in my stuff and I won't snoop in yours. Got that?"

Jorja swallowed around her suddenly tight throat. "Sure. Whatever."

Ashley got up. "Well, good. Now that we have an understanding things should be much more pleasant around here, shouldn't they?"

Jorja flounced out of the kitchen without a word.

Ashley breathed a sigh of relief. When it rained it poured for her. It seemed as if every five years she had a load of drama to deal with. She stood with her elbow on the counter and looked through the window unseeingly.

Ruel's sermon was ringing in her head. *Consequences to Sin...* she was reaping what she had sown. She should take it like a man.

Chapter Five

Bible study was well attended. Lyn had told her to show up at seven o'clock because that was the time they usually started but Regina had reasoned that nobody would show up that early for something so boring. She was surprised to see that she was wrong and the group was large. About thirty persons attended and they were sitting together on one side of the church. She would have to join them and be in the thick of things. Somehow she had imagined that it would be more like a church service so that she could slip into the back unnoticed.

Unfortunately, when she got to the group she saw that they were just welcoming everybody and she was asked to introduce herself and tell her name and where she was from. She felt like telling them to mind their own business.

She stood though, looking over the group with her best fake smile on. Ashley was sitting beside her husband in the front. She was not smiling. Her husband looked grim too and was looking at her intently.

And then there were the Kincaids. They were sitting behind the pastor. Norma Kincaid was giving her an intense assessing look as well, as if she were mentally scanning her for information.

Regina suddenly felt chilled.

She dragged her eyes from Norma's and met the eyes of her son, Jack. He had his mother's eyes, but while Norma's looked normal, his were bordering on the sinister, as if he had judged her and found her wanting.

Regina shook off the sense of foreboding. She was being fanciful. These people didn't know her. She knew them and what they were up to. She was the one with the upper hand. Not them.

"Don't be shy." The kindly church sister who looked like a dark version of Sofia from the Golden Girls, said gently, "You are among friends, dear."

Regina cleared her throat; none of that statement was true. She was not shy nor was she among friends.

"Well, I, er...my name is Regina Tharwick and I am on a, er, vacation up here and I am here to learn..."

"Good. Welcome," the old lady said, genuinely pleased to see her.

Regina was hoping to sit down at the very back but Josiah Coke was waving to her from the third row and was pointing to an empty spot beside him.

"She is my invitee," he announced proudly.

"Ah," the lady at the front said, smiling. "Good job, Brother Josiah. We should all do the same and invite others to join us every night. Are there any other visitors?"

A young girl stood up. She was on the other side of the bench that Regina was forced to sit in because of the overeager Josiah. The girl had long braids, almost to her waist, and she looked almost as out of place as Regina knew she looked.

She was in makeup and her dress was at least two inches above her knees. Plus she had a piece of jewelry on her thumb. Regina chuckled to herself, wondering who had succeeded in pulling her out of her house for the study.

"My name is Jorja Dennison," the girl said. Her voice was low and husky.

"Welcome Jorja," the lady at the front said pleasantly. "We hear that you are with us for longer than the summer. We are glad to have you. Our pastor and Sister Ashley must be pleased that you are around. We really don't consider you to be a visitor; you are a part of us."

That was when it dawned on Regina that this girl that stood out like a sore thumb, almost as badly as she did, was Ruel's daughter. She wished now that she had King check her out. The home situation was going to be volatile with her in it. She was sure that Jorja wouldn't be pleased to have Ashley as a stepmother.

Another reason why Ashley should see sense and leave with her for Kingston.

"Tonight, we are honored to have our new associate pastor, Nolan Ramsey, conduct Bible study." The old lady leading out said, "Welcome pastor."

The associate pastor got up and turned to the group. He was young, maybe in his early twenties, average-looking, with a little goatee. It bothered Regina that she had not known about him or else she would have had King check him out too. Or maybe she should check him out herself. She had nothing but time on her hands. It wouldn't hurt to do some sleuthing.

Nolan Ramsey. His name seemed vaguely familiar, the more she thought about it. She rifled in her mind as to why that was and almost missed the first half of his presentation, which was a pity. He seemed enthusiastic and sincere.

He was looking at the story of Jonah.

Regina was totally unfamiliar with the story or that it was even a book in the Bible. It sounded interesting enough, though. It was like a little fairytale to her. A man living in a fish for three days was next to impossible, wasn't it?

She was surprised at that thought, especially since she believed that the Bible study was going to be boring. She was glancing over at Josiah's open Bible to see if what Nolan was talking about was true. He slyly pushed it into her lap inch-by-inch until she was holding it.

Regina glanced at him to let him know that she knew what he was doing but then changed her mind. Norma Kincaid spun around and looked from her to the Bible in approval.

Regina almost laughed out loud. Was that all it took to be a part of this crazy bunch of people, pretend to read the Bible?

They were all a bunch of pretenders, from Ashley to her pastor husband and all the other people in between.

*****

"Nolan certainly seems capable, doesn't he?" Ruel said when they got into the car after the Bible study.

"He's kinda boring," Jorja mumbled. "Do I have to do this every night?"

"Yes," Ruel said, his voice brooking no argument.

Ashley was in deep contemplation. She was not paying attention to Ruel and Jorja. Regina was planning something; she could feel it. Before they drove out of the church yard she could see her leaning on her car and conversing with a group of people. As usual, she was quite animated.

"I wonder what she is telling them," Ashley whispered

before Ruel started the car.

"Who knows?" Ruel's voice was grim.

"You see the danger of having her here now?" Ashley asked.

"Oh yes," Ruel said tensely. "I see that she can cause havoc if left to her own devices."

"I like her," Jorja said from the back seat. "She looks cool. That tattoo on her cheek--is it a bow?"

"Stay away from her." Ruel started the car and glanced back at his daughter.

Ashley sighed. Ruel shouldn't have said that. From what she knew about Jorja, she was going to do the opposite. She only thought Regina was cool because Ashley obviously disliked her. She only hoped that Regina wouldn't give Jorja any ammunition against her.

"Maybe I should hear what she has to say. Maybe then I can learn her motives for being up here," Ashley said after they were driving in silence for a while.

"No!" Ruel said quickly. "Definitely not!"

"But why not?" Ashley frowned. Ruel was looking unusually agitated.

"I'll talk to her." Ruel squeezed the steering wheel tighter. "I am your husband. I'll deal with it."

"Okay," Ashley said, "thanks honey. You know you are the best. I hope Regina will see reason."

Ruel squeezed her hand briefly and then released it.

*****

"Regina Tharwick." Norma Kincaid made her way towards her daintily. The small crowd that surrounded her parted for her to have access to Regina. "I hear from Josiah that you played for the national football team. It is lovely to meet you."

She held out her hand for a handshake and Regina took it reluctantly.

"So, what brings you to our neck of the woods?" Norma asked softly. Regina realized that this was no polite inquiry. The lady was looking at her with a healthy dose of suspicion.

"Peace and quiet." She repeated the lie she had been spouting for the past couple of days.

"Ah," Norma said but she wasn't buying it. Her son, Jack, came ambling over to them. He stood behind his mother and stared fixedly at Regina.

"Well, er, I should go," Regina said. "I'll be back for Bible class tomorrow."

"Good," Norma said. "Nice to know that in your search for peace and quiet you are finding time for God."

"Yes." Regina couldn't meet her eyes after that statement. She started searching for the car key in her bag.

"By the way," Norma moved even closer to her and gave the persons who were closest to them a look. When she did this they drifted away as if by tacit consent. Even Josiah, who looked like he was eager to say something to her, followed the group obediently. The queen bee could do that with only a look. Amazing.

Regina found her key and clutched it, forced to look up at Norma Kincaid who seemed ridiculously tall compared to her.

"Do you know a Kingsley Harper?"

Regina stiffened. King! What did Norma know about King?

"I see that you do." Norma walked even closer to Regina. She towered over her. She was smiling but the smile did not reach her eyes.

"What are you up to, Regina?" Norma spoke normally but

Regina could feel the menace underneath the words.

"Nothing." Regina forced her feet to stay where they were. She felt like backing up to her car. She was feeling irrationally fearful and was ready to flee.

"Who sent you up here?" Norma was not backing down. "Who would dare to do such a thing?"

"I don't know what you are talking about?" Regina's voice trembled and it sounded convincing even to her own ears.

Norma pulled back from Regina and studied her in the half dark for a few tension-filled seconds.

"Well then, looking forward to seeing you tomorrow night. I will be conducting the study."

Regina got into her car and breathed out shakily. When she turned on her headlights she could see Jack standing behind his mother. His pale face looked almost ghostly when the light surrounded him. His hands were in his pockets in a deceptively relaxed pose and his shoulders were hunched over. He was staring at her in that weird, menacing manner of his.

Maybe, just maybe, she had bitten off a bit more than she could chew up here in Primrose Hill. She reversed from the churchyard, her hands not quite steady.

Chapter Six

The morning after the church yard fiasco with Norma Kincaid, Regina was unsure about what she should do. She glanced at the files spread around her. She had taken them out and read them again, especially the ones about Norma Kincaid. She should call the police, reveal what she knew, and leave them to it.

Her suitcase was opened in the corner; she hadn't even bothered to unpack it. All she needed to do was pick up her toiletries scattered on the bathroom counter, put on her clothes and get out of here. Forget Ashley and the two of them getting back together. Then she groaned.

How could she forget Ashley? She couldn't in all good conscience allow her to stay in her relationship with Ruel. She was almost sure that Ruel was less than honest with Ashley about his past. She grabbed his file and looked it over again. When she first read it she had wondered if King was mistaken.

Ruel Dennison, forty years old, minister of the gospel, up until one year and two months ago married to Rosalie Dennison Nee Miller. They had a volatile marriage. Ruel's mother Miriam Dennison described them as the worst pairing in the history of pairings.

Rosalie was an abuser, not the easiest of wives to handle, often becoming violent to her husband in public settings. Regina sat back with the file on her lap and couldn't quite imagine it. She had to give it to Ruel, he had not lifted a finger to defend himself against his wife.

However, the next part of the report had her shaking her head in fear for Ashley. Ruel and Rosalie had taken a vacation together to Florida and Rosalie died in a car accident. Ruel had been driving but had not gotten a scratch from the accident.

He conveniently had her body cremated and then he returned to Jamaica with an urn full of Rosalie's ashes, where they had a thanksgiving service for her life.

One week later he was at a convention and met Ashley. Six weeks later they were married.

There was no grieving for his first wife; in fact, her friends said that it was the happiest they had ever seen him. His wife's passing had not even caused a ripple in his existence. It was too pat, too convenient. Ruel had something to hide. Regina was almost sure that he killed Rosalie and was getting away with it.

She laid back down on her pillow and looked up at the ceiling contemplatively. Ashley was so defensive she probably wouldn't listen if she told her anything about her precious Ruel. She was still under the delusion that he was the epitome of love and goodwill. They were probably still in their honeymoon phase where she had her rose-colored glasses fixed firmly to her face.

But Regina vowed she would not leave until Ashley heard the full story. She was sure if Ashley had heard what really happened she would not have married Ruel. Her sense of preservation would kick in and she would know better than to get herself involved in such a fishy situation.

She glanced at her clock—too late now to catch Ashley walking, but she could take a stroll outside. She had passed a house at the bottom of the hill that stood out because of its garden. It had some lovely flowers. Maybe she could photograph some of them.

*****

When she reached the bottom of the hill she saw a tall young man watering the plants and singing *Something Inside So Strong* at the top of his voice. *The more you refuse to hear my voice, the louder I will sing.* He belted that part out and Regina slowed down and grinned. She was disappointed that she would not be able to take pictures but she was finding his antics of watering the plants and singing quite entertaining.

He saw her and stopped singing. She hadn't wanted him to do that.

"Hello," he called out chirpily and waved.

Regina drifted closer to the white picket fence and smiled. "Hello. I wanted to take some pictures of your plants. They are beautiful; the only green place in this drought."

"You can come in. My mom would be flattered that you like her plants enough to take pictures. If people are not impressed enough by them she finds some way to bring them up in conversations. So take as many pictures as you want."

"How are they so green, though?" Regina asked, crouching down beside a deep violet shrub and positioning her camera at the perfect spot.

"We water the plants with water from Rose Hill farms fish ponds. Uncle Conroy carries water from there for my mom every morning."

"Oh." Regina took her eyes away from the camera and squinted up at him. She supposed that this was Oliver Allen.

She had a very interesting dossier on his mother, Honey Allen, registered nurse, manager of the only clinic in the district.

"Interesting isn't it?" Oliver asked her, thinking that she was impressed by the fish water explanation.

"Yes, very interesting." Regina cleared her throat. "What's your name?"

"Oliver Allen." He grinned. "And you need no introduction. You are the girl baller, Regina Tharwick."

Regina frowned. "News travels fast around here."

"Yes." Oliver nodded. He finished watering his section of the garden and came closer to her. "Josiah told me that you were staying up here. I have never met a girl who plays football before."

Regina grinned. "A girl? That's very flattering, Oliver, but though I look like a fresh young chicken, I am really a tough old hen."

Oliver laughed, his eyes sparkling in mirth. He was a handsome lad, maybe what the little girls in high school would call cute and whisper in the corners about. His hair was in curly ringlets across his head. Some of them were long enough they were almost in his eyes. He raked them away with his free hand and they came right back. The style should look feminine but didn't, not on him.

"What was it like playing football on the national stage?" He grinned again and Regina got the sensation that she had seen that exact same grin just yesterday morning on Josiah Coke.

They even had the same way of holding their heads. Oliver was waiting for her to say something about playing football but for the life of her she was shell-shocked. Why would he remind her of Josiah Coke? What was the story here?

And once the thought took root that indeed there was a story there, it wouldn't go away. They didn't look much alike. Josiah was taller than average, whipcord lean and had a longish, straight face. This boy, Oliver, was average height and had a square face, a little cleft in his chin, all that curly Indian hair...

"Excuse me," Honey called from the veranda. She was in a bright green and voluminous caftan dress. Her long hair hung to her hips in black, snaky tendrils. "Who are you?"

Regina dragged her eyes from Oliver's face and concentrated on his mother. Oliver looked like her and she was aptly named honey. Her brown, smooth skin was the shade of orange blossom honey.

"Hi, I am Regina." She pointed to the flowers. "I was just admiring your flowers and Oliver said it was okay for me to take pictures."

Honey looked at her unsmilingly. "Okay."

Obviously not impressed by the explanation, she folded her arms and looked at Regina as if waiting for something else.

Regina searched in her mind for something to say. "It is a lovely area."

"It's fine. We could do with some rain," Honey said, her voice slightly warmer. "We have a river about a half mile down the road but it is almost dry."

"Completely dry. No water at all," Oliver murmured beside her. "It even has a waterfall. People go down there and swim when it has water. It's a pity you won't see it when it is flowing. You could take some pictures."

"I could still take some pictures," Regina said, smiling. "Even dry river beds have their beauty."

"I could show you where it is," Oliver said, putting down his watering can.

Regina nodded. "Would you? That would be so nice of you." And then she added for his mother's benefit, "I must say, the people in this community are so welcoming and Christian-like."

Oliver flushed at the compliment. "It's just how we are."

Honey abandoned her folded-arm stance and the hostility fell from her. She stood back, looking at her son. "When you come back you have the flowers in the greenhouse to take care of."

"Yes Mom." Oliver nodded.

"Well, have a nice day, Regina." Honey's voice was much warmer now.

Regina smiled. "Thank you, Mrs. er..." she stammered, deliberately pretending that she didn't know Honey's name.

"Honey Allen," Honey said pleasantly. "You can call me Honey."

*****

"Very well-played," Oliver said when they were out of earshot of his mother.

"What are you talking about?" Regina feigned innocence.

"You compliment her flowers, the neighborhood, you throw in Christianity and she's like putty in your hands."

Regina looked at him, surprised at how astute he was. "I am not admitting to anything."

Oliver chuckled. "You never did answer me about what it was like playing for the national team. You went into a little trance, staring at me, until my mother broke it up."

Regina stopped walking and looked at him. "How old are you?"

Oliver raised an eyebrow. "I am flattered, Miss Tharwick, by the question but I may seem like an old rooster but I really am a spring chicken."

Regina laughed, unexpectedly surprised at his quick wit and sharp intelligence.

"I am seventeen." Oliver folded his arms and looked at her. "How old are you?"

"Thirty-five." Regina smirked. "I am old enough to be your mother."

"I don't doubt it," Oliver grinned, "and I wasn't flirting. Besides, with your hairstyle and tattoos and masculine trod, I am going to assume you are not into my gender."

Regina squinted at him. "Now, now, that's quite an assumption."

"Yup." Oliver nodded. "I am guessing that's the right assumption too."

Regina started walking. "So tell me about Primrose Hill. You are so observant I am guessing that you are the right source of information about this place."

"You could say that." Oliver reached into his pocket for an elastic band and pulled his hair back into a ponytail.

"And you won't go blabbing to anyone that I asked you?" Regina looked at him.

"Nope. I don't blab." Oliver shrugged. "There is nobody to blab to. I am basically a loner. My mom made sure of that. She's, er, how would you put it?"

"Overprotective?"

Oliver chuckled. "That's my mom."

"Where's your dad?" Regina put the camera to her eyes and pretended that she was interested in capturing a bird perched on a branch.

"My dad is gone. Last my mom heard he was in Barbados, but she doesn't really know. He left when I was a baby. I don't remember a thing about him. My mom doesn't even have a picture. Uncle Conroy is more of a dad to me."

Regina lowered the camera and looked at him quizzically. "That's Conroy Coke, the guy with the farm?"

"Yes." Oliver grinned. "You really don't do pretending that well."

"What on earth do you mean?" Regina lifted the camera again.

"You want to know about my parents and their relationship and if my mom has a guy in her life."

"Well, yes." Regina nodded. "Is she with Conroy Coke?"

"Maybe." Oliver shrugged. "They are pretty close. Every morning he carries water for Mom's flowers in the back of his truck. She cooks breakfast for him. They talk a lot on the phone..."

"Okay," Regina spun around and looked at him fully, "have you ever given thought to the fact that he is your real father?"

Oliver laughed and then he sobered up. "No. That would be pretty impossible."

"How impossible?"

"Well, I am seventeen," Oliver said patiently, "which means they would have met up what, eighteen years ago. Eighteen years ago both of them were married to other people."

Regina snorted. "Were they both in Jamaica?"

"Yes." Oliver was looking uncomfortable now.

"Where?"

"In Kingston," Oliver said faintly. "My mom was a nurse at the University Hospital and Uncle Conroy was working as a police detective at some place or the other in Kingston too."

"And..." Regina prompted.

"And nothing." Oliver frowned. "They are not the kind of people to sneak around and have affairs. My mother is so, so..."

"Perfect," Regina said, "holier than thou."

Oliver looked at Regina contemplatively. "And Uncle Conroy is..."

"The church police and a strict vegetarian," Regina grinned, "therefore they must not have had sexual relations."

Oliver frowned but didn't say anything to that.

"Never underestimate the drama potential of country folks," Regina said softly. "People are people wherever they are."

"Why are you really here, Regina?" Oliver asked, frowning.

"To make someone see sense and come back home with me," Regina answered promptly. "Speaking of returning home, when did your uncle Conroy come back to this place?"

"Seven…eight years ago," Oliver said. He was obviously troubled. He ran his hand through his hair, dislodging the band that was holding it back.

"And when did your mother come back?"

"Around the same time." Oliver had all but slowed down. He stumbled slightly and then sat on a rock at the side of the road and put his hand on his head.

"Coincidence," Regina murmured, "strange coincidence. Your father disappearing without contacting you. Conroy's wife leaving him and now they are back in the same district where they grew up together."

"They were childhood sweethearts," Oliver said weakly. "My mom's parents were against them getting together because he is older than her, so they split them up. Both sets of parents are dead now, so when they returned to Primrose Hill they could hang out freely."

"I wonder why they don't just get married, because here you are, their love child of years past." Regina grinned. "Quite a story."

"It's not true." Oliver stood up and brushed himself off. "My mom would not lie to me for so long about something so important. Besides, she is very much against premarital sex, extramarital sex—well, sex in general."

"Suit yourself if you want to believe that. Obviously, she must have been into sex at some point." Regina shrugged. "Tell me about Norma Kincaid."

"What about her?" Oliver asked warily.

"She scares me," Regina said after a pause.

Oliver laughed. "Aunty Norma is nice."

"Nice, huh?" Regina shuddered. "She's really not nice. She is the queen of naughty."

Oliver breathed a sigh of relief when they reached the dry river bed after Regina's statement about his precious Aunty Norma.

"I don't think I want to hear anything else." Oliver massaged his head.

"Not even about your pastor? I have something juicy on him."

"Good God, no!" Oliver said shakily. "You have suspicions about Pastor Ruel too?"

"Oh yes," Regina said grimly. "I have suspicions about everybody and I am pretty sure I am right."

Oliver looked at her, astonishment lighting his eyes. "But why?"

"Because I told you I want back what is rightfully mine."

"What is rightfully yours?" Oliver shook his head. "I thought you said that you want somebody to come back home with you."

"I do," Regina said, determined. "And she is rightfully

mine."

"She? You say that as if this she is a possession." Oliver frowned. "Who could this person be?"

"You'll work it out." Regina grinned. "Because I am pretty sure she'll be coming back with me soon. Until she comes home, there will not be any rest for the people at your church and their bag of secrets."

*****

Oliver returned home a little after ten. Regina had found the dry riverbed fascinating and she had changed the subject from secrets and cover-ups to football, a move calculated to make him feel more at ease, and it had worked. He watched as she walked up the hill, her camera swinging, and then he walked toward the greenhouse.

His mother would be long gone to work by now and he had the rest of the day to himself after he watered the plants.

He realized that he didn't want the rest of the day to think; Regina's little theory had stuck in his head and was whirring around like a whirlpool. He was convinced that Regina was totally wrong about his mother and Conroy Coke but he couldn't help but think, what if?

What if she was right?

His hand trembled on the water can and he put it down. His mother would not do what Regina was suggesting, nor would Conroy Coke. It was ridiculous, preposterous and downright crazy.

He was Oliver Allen. His real father was Tony Allen, medical doctor. His mother described him as tall, squarish face, a quiet person who had depression issues.

He might not know him personally because he was too young when he left but he was still the donor of biological material to his DNA. Not anyone else. To even entertain such thoughts was madness.

He imagined his mother shaking her head at him and confirming it. *Madness Oliver, trite speculation by a stranger who doesn't know your family or the values they stand for.*

He left the water can in the middle of the greenhouse and then headed inside. He hadn't been this curious about his father in years. His mother had a grainy photo that she had showed him some time ago but it had disappeared since then and she was so defensive about talking about Tony Allen that it was not really worth it to bring him up in conversation.

He needed a distraction, something, anything to take his mind off this loop it was on. He didn't have any distractions at home. His mother was distrustful of the television and when the last one broke down four years ago she did not replace it. She was also distrustful of computers and the Internet.

He had gotten a laptop from the Kincaids for his birthday last year and he had gleefully watched as his mom tried hard not to refuse it. She was afraid of rubbing Norma Kincaid the wrong way.

Knowing the power she wielded, Norma had given him the opportunity to come to her house to use the Internet anytime he wanted.

He showered and pulled on his blue jeans and a purple t-shirt which could use some ironing but he was disturbed enough to not stop and get that done. He grabbed his laptop, pushed it in his bag and hoped that when he reached the Kincaids' house Jack would be there. They usually played against each other in various video games. He had stopped playing a year ago but he really needed not to think today.

Two things struck Oliver when he rode up into the Kincaid's yard. Pastor Ruel was in a whispered conversation with Aunty Norma in the middle of the driveway and the driver side of his car door was opened. A girl was sitting in the passenger side, her jean clad feet on the dashboard.

"Hello," he called to her, leaning down near the car so that he could see her better.

She dragged her feet off the dashboard and sat up straighter in the seat.

"Hi."

She was pretty. A real girly-girl type. She had long box braids in her hair and a pink band around it and she was in matching pink accessories.

He grinned. "It must be hot out here."

"Yes it is," she grinned back, "but I decided to follow my dad on his visits today."

"Pastor Ruel's your dad?" Oliver grinned. "Then you must be Jorja."

"Yes." She smiled. "And you are?"

"Oliver." He straightened up and then looked over at Pastor Ruel, who hadn't shifted since he rode up. Aunty Norma was saying something to him in a strident voice, as if she was distressed. Oliver wondered what that was about.

He leaned back down and looked into the car. "Want to hang with me and Jack? We usually play video games."

She nodded eagerly. "Sure."

When she got out of the car and slammed the door, Pastor Ruel still hadn't shifted. He was so engrossed in the conversation that when he neared them, neither adult even acknowledged them.

He slowed down and almost stopped when he heard Aunty Norma whisper hoarsely, "We need to do something about that woman, Ruel. You and I both know that she cannot stay up here. She had me investigated. I should have known that something was wrong when she came here out of the blue and then King followed. I know King; he has become a well-known private investigator..."

"Hey Dad," Jorja said behind the conversing adults. "I am going to hang with Oliver and Jack today."

Pastor Ruel looked around at the both of them a little dazedly. "Yes, sure dear."

Oliver smiled at both of them. "Pastor, Aunty Norma."

He knew something was seriously wrong when his normally chirpy aunty gave him a vague smile and a nod. "Have fun, dears."

Pastor Ruel nodded as if in agreement and they went back to whispering. When Oliver looked behind, Pastor Ruel was cupping the back of his neck in a nervous gesture. And then Oliver remembered Regina saying that she had secrets about him and Aunty Norma.

He didn't want to jump to conclusions but he was almost sure that the person who Aunty Norma said couldn't stay up here would be Regina.

But maybe that was a stretch and he was seeing intrigue where none existed.

*****

Uncle Owen was in the den in his special big chair, his laptop on a table beside him. Jack was sitting before the television with a video game controller already in hand.

The den was a huge cavernous basement room that they used as their recreational area. It was air conditioned and had a fridge which was stocked with several types of drinks but most importantly of all they had WiFi Internet.

"I brought company," Oliver announced when he got downstairs.

"Wow!" Jorja whispered beside him, looking around.

There were game tables and sitting areas and two televisions, one of which was dedicated to playing games.

"Come on in," Uncle Owen looked up from his perusal of the computer and smiled when he saw Jorja.

He got up and lumbered toward them. "Mi casa is su casa, especially to pretty ladies."

He shook Jorja's hands and slapped Oliver on his back in his usual jovial manner. "I am working from home today."

Oliver nodded. He liked Uncle Owen. Sometimes when they wanted a third man for their games he would jump in.

He owned a employment placement business in the town. Some days he didn't go into the office because he wasn't needed. It must be nice being rich.

Jack looked up from his place on the floor and grunted and then turned around.

"He likes you," Oliver said, grinning. "Jack only grunts at people he likes."

Jorja grimaced but she sat beside Jack and took up the game controls.

"You are a girl," Jack said abruptly.

"Congrats for stating the obvious but girl or not, I can beat you," Jorja said, a challenge in her voice.

Jack grunted again.

Owen guffawed. "Be careful Jack, she's a fiery one."

Jack smirked and the faintest of smiles crossed his pale lips. Jack had an issue being in social situations. He rarely smiled for anybody and only a privileged few persons heard him speak.

He was extremely close to Aunty Norma, who still treated him like a child, and in some respects he was. Jack was a slow developer and notoriously shy even at twenty-four.

Oliver had no idea how the rumor began that Jack smoked marijuana and it messed up his brain. Though Aunty Norma caught him with a joint a couple of years ago, it hadn't even been lit.

Oliver told his mother this time and time again but she always chose to believe that Jack was a drug junkie or something. Nobody seemed to want to accept that he was just slow or developmentally challenged.

Oliver watched them for a while and saw that Jorja was holding her own against Jack, whose fingers were flying over the game controls like a pro. He went for his laptop and sat across from Uncle Owen and turned on his computer.

He had to do some research on Regina. There must be stuff about her on the Internet; maybe he could find a clue as to who this person was that she just had to take back to Kingston with her.

And he would research his father too. He wanted to know where he was. Maybe get some contact information for him and find out why he had disappeared out of his life.

"So what about summer jobs?" Owen asked before he could click an Internet link. "Are you getting one this summer?"

Oliver grimaced. "Yes, the usual. I am going to work with Josiah at the farm office again. I am going by there today to let him know when I'll be ready to start."

"Good." Owen nodded. "That's more than some people have, you know."

"I guess," Oliver said, waiting for the Internet browser to open. He typed in: Regina Jamaican Footballer, and saw quite a few pages on her, even a picture.

Her name was Regina Tharwick and they used to call her the pit bull. Most of the articles were old, though, and they only dealt with her career. There was nothing about her life after football or any relationships.

He chuckled at the headline, The Pit bull Strikes Again. It had a picture of a much younger looking Regina in her football outfit, clutching a ball to her chest.

He could understand why Regina was referred to as the pit bull. He spent just a few minutes in her company and had gotten the feeling that she was indeed that kind of person.

He wondered afresh who the woman was that Regina declared was hers and that she was not leaving till she came home with her. He tried to think about who it could be but it totally slipped him. All the people he knew were heterosexual, or he thought they were. One could never tell these days.

"You look to be in deep thought." Owen jerked him out of his reverie.

Oliver smiled. "I have a couple of things on my mind."

He typed in his dad's name, Tony Allen, doctor, and couldn't find anything on him. He tried university hospital, he tried the year that his mother said she met him at the hospital, but he came up with nothing.

"Is there a place where you can check for registered medical doctors?" Oliver asked Owen hesitantly.

He didn't want Uncle Owen asking him what for? He didn't want anybody to know that he was now laboring under some really mammoth doubts about his paternity.

"Yes." Owen nodded without question and told him the web address for a medical licensing website.

He checked for Tony Allen and came up with zilch, nada. Tony Allen didn't exist, or at least was not practicing medicine legally in Jamaica or elsewhere.

"I think you would make a fine doctor," Owen murmured. He was typing something rapidly on his computer too and he said it almost absently.

Oliver grimaced. "My mother wants me to be a doctor. I am not sure I want that. She's obsessed with it because that is what she wanted to do and according to her she missed the boat."

"Mmmm," Owen looked at him briefly, "give it a chance. Maybe in this case mother knows best."

"We can't afford med school and all of that right now." Oliver shrugged, "I think I should just do something that is easier and will get me earning in a short time span."

Owen nodded. "I get it, you want to be responsible and be a provider but some things should be done when you are young, when your body can stand under the pressure.

"Sometimes I wish that Norma and I had started branching out into other businesses when we were much younger. Besides, you could do so much with a medical degree.

"You could go on those medical missionary trips to Africa that your mother keeps insisting that you are going to do."

"That's her dream." Oliver sighed. "My mother has a one-track mind when it comes to her dreams for me. I can't even get in a word edgewise when she outlines her plans for my life."

Jorja looked around at them; obviously she was half-listening to their conversation. "My dad wants me to be a teacher or something but I am going to be a superstar, like Alicia Keys. I can sing like her and I desperately want to learn to play the piano too."

Owen smiled. "You have that kind of voice, huh? With your face and a killer voice I would say your dad will probably be disappointed when you become a superstar instead of a teacher. If you desperately want to learn to play the piano I can arrange that with the guy who taught Jack."

Jorja grinned shyly. "Thanks Mr. Kincaid."

"No, no, not Mr. Kincaid, Uncle Owen. Everybody calls me that. Besides, your dad and I grew up together right here in Primrose hill. We were like brothers. Though obviously I was a little older."

Jorja spun around, losing the game in the process. "Tell me about my dad. When he was a boy, what was he like?"

Jack grunted in triumph but Jorja ignored him, her eyes fixed on Owen.

"Your dad was really skinny," Owen laughed, "and though he was half the size of the big boys he would always want to hang out with us. He could out-dive any of us in the rivers and he always seemed to catch more fish when we went fishing."

Jorja laughed. "That's nice. Did you know my mom?"

Owen's grin faded. "Unfortunately, no. Ruel left here and went to college and moved on with his life. Norma and I left here too, for a little while. We only recently crossed paths when he came back to the district."

Jorja's grin disappeared as quickly as she had lit up.

Norma walked into the room. She was acting more jittery than normal.

"Owen, come along," she said abruptly, "leave the young people to have fun."

Owen got up promptly. "Coming, dear."

"I should go too." Oliver stood up. Being at the Kincaid's was not proving to be the distraction he had envisioned it to be. He couldn't spend time playing video games now that he had more questions about his father since Regina filled his head with her theories.

"I am coming with you, Oliver!" Jorja jumped up swiftly. "I am hanging with you today."

"Okay." Oliver pushed his laptop into his bag. "I am going to the farm. Are you sure that you don't want to stay and hang with Jack?"

Jorja shook her head vigorously and trailed behind him as he headed out the door.

Jack ignored them and started another game without

acknowledging that they told him goodbye.

Chapter Seven

"He's creepy," Jorja said as soon as they exited the Kincaid's house and were heading down the road toward Rose Hill Farm.

"Who?" Oliver glanced at her. He was looking down at the top of her head. She was about five feet flat.

"Jack!" Jorja looked at him and giggled. "Owen is nice though, very cute."

Oliver quirked his brow. "Uncle Owen? I can understand you thinking that Jack is creepy but Uncle Owen is old. Old people are not cute and especially not in that tone of voice."

Jorja laughed. "I like older men."

Oliver shook his head. "Okay then. He's a grandfather; his oldest child has a child."

Jorja flicked her braid over her shoulders. "So?"

"So..." Oliver said in exasperation, "I am not having this conversation with you. It is ridiculous anyway."

"Are you jealous?" Jorja asked slyly.

Oliver paused and looked at her. He wasn't attracted to her. She was pretty and shapely but he just wasn't moved. Besides, her thinking that his Uncle Owen was cute had left a bad taste in his mouth. He found that kind of joke distasteful, even if she was trying to make him jealous.

"No, I am not jealous," Oliver said abruptly. "I just met you. How can I be jealous? Are you sure you want to come with me to the farm?"

"Sure, why not," Jorja said sulkily. "You know you are really cute too, don't you?"

Oliver shrugged. "Thanks, I guess."

"Are we going to be in the same class when I go back to school?"

"No. I skipped a couple of years. This is my last year and then university. I figure you'll be in fifth form or something."

"Yes or they'll have me repeat. I am pretty sure I flunked my exams last term."

"Why?" Oliver asked her.

She scrunched up her face in a moue. "Because my mother died and one week after my father came back with her ashes he had a service and then packed up the house. Two lousy months later he got married to the beauty queen and then left me to live with Grandma Miriam, who was almost as bad as my mom."

"You had an issue with your mom?" Oliver put his laptop bag on the bar of the bicycle and slowed his steps to match Jorja's.

"Oh yes." Jorja looked as if she was contemplating telling him more about her mom and then decided against it. "It was always just me and my dad, even when my mother was there; that's why it hurt so bad when he left me with Grandma."

"Sorry," Oliver said sympathetically. "But look on the bright side, you are back home with him now."

"But the beauty queen is there too," Jorja bemoaned. "And she is not nice. I just met you and you seem nicer than she is."

Oliver glanced at her. "Sis Ashley seems pretty nice to me. She seems like she would be a cool stepmother. Maybe you should give her a chance. She was my business teacher last term. She's really good. Everybody likes her."

"I would give her a chance as you put it but," Jorja sighed as if the weight of the world was on her shoulders, "she doesn't like me. As it is, I am going to have to sleep with one eye open. I heard her telling Dad that there was a lady up here that was creating trouble for her and she wishes that she would disappear off the face of the earth. Apparently they were former friends. Can you believe that? And I heard her calling the lady obsessed and evil. I think that is the way she thinks about me."

Oliver stopped walking. He looked at his watch. It was nearly eleven-thirty and the day was scorchingly hot already. He wheeled his bicycle under a tree and leaned it up on one of the scraggly trunks and then he closed his eyes.

Jorja followed him and stood looking at him curiously. "You okay?"

"No," Oliver croaked. "I might have a little bit more information running around in my head than I can process right now."

Jorja shrugged and sat on the tree trunk a little distance from him.

"Like what?"

"Ah," Oliver rubbed his temples, "just some stuff."

"Is the farm far from here?"

"No. No," Oliver answered, "about five minutes from here."

"What do they have there?"

"Give me a second." Oliver squeezed his eyes shut. Ashley Dennison, the pastor's wife, was the reason Regina was up here.

Ashley Dennison!

His mind allowed that to simmer for a while. Regina said she had dirt on everyone, including Pastor Ruel. She also said that Pastor Ruel had secrets and that Norma Kincaid was naughty, not nice.

He had a total recall memory. Once it was said he could bring it back to mind verbatim. And Regina's conversation was running through his head now, and he didn't like the dots that he was connecting.

He also heard Aunty Norma today with Pastor Ruel, saying that Regina couldn't stay.

So if he had any sense at all, and he liked to think he had a fair share, he would conclude that Regina was indeed holding secrets and she had Norma Kincaid afraid.

The most shocking info of all was that Ashley Dennison was her ex-lover.

He swallowed when he thought of that. Could that be true?

If Regina had secrets on everybody maybe his mother had secrets too. He couldn't ignore that. Maybe Regina's musings about his paternity were right.

The urge to know more was suddenly stifling.

He inhaled raggedly. He didn't know what to do with all of the information that he had gained today. Who could he talk to about this?

He cracked his eye open and looked at Jorja. She took a pack of gum from her pants pocket and held it out. "Want one?"

"No thanks," Oliver said hoarsely.

Definitely not her. He didn't really know her, did he, and if he shared anything about his speculations, especially if it had to do with Ashley, she would probably blab about it as soon as she reached home.

"It will make you think better," Jorja offered sweetly, wiggling the gum like it was some cure-all for what ailed him.

What he wanted was an adult he could trust. That used to be his mother, but today he was rethinking that. Maybe she had been lying to him for years.

"No." Oliver straightened up from the bicycle. "Sorry about that. I have a lot on my mind."

Jorja giggled. "Don't we all. Ready?"

"Yes." Oliver nodded. "Sure."

*****

Oliver visited Rose Hill farms so often that he rarely took stock of his surroundings. Right now was different, though. Because of Regina and her speculations he was seeing everything with new suspicion.

He looked at the sign. It was a freshly painted wooden sign. The logo had a cabbage where the O in Rose should be. It had the word welcome underneath it. For years the welcome had been misspelled and it used to drive his mother crazy.

Conroy would laugh when she mentioned it. He was fine with it. He called it a landmark but when Josiah came back from Kingston, he had changed the sign, updated the buildings, hired more help, and expanded the business to include three more greenhouses.

In the space of a year Rose Hill Farm had changed from a limping one-man operation to a major supplier of vegetables and fish. Last summer when he worked with Josiah, he had gotten a ton load of work to do and Josiah had paid him over and above what he thought a regular kid should get.

Conroy probably told Josiah to top up his summer salary out of guilt because he was his secret dad!

He looked over at the vast twelve acres to the mango trees in the distance and the several transparent greenhouses where rows and rows of greenery could be clearly seen and the surrounding mini-fish ponds, which supplied the greenhouses with water.

He could see Conroy near the ponds talking to someone and gesticulating in a rapid manner. Somebody must have gotten him roiled up; Conroy was usually placid, not given to excess emotions unless it came to Honey. When he was around her he became a different man.

Oliver dragged his mind from that train of thought and went back to admiring the land. To the left of the gate was what looked like a ranch house but it had a sign that said office. That was where Josiah and Conroy had their offices, and a mini-store where they sold seeds and farming supplies. That is where he would find Josiah now. He needed to talk to him about his summer job.

"This place is awesome!" Jorja grinned. "Really awesome and huge. I didn't expect this. Are those bell peppers in pots at the front? They plant them like flowers. Can we go into the green houses?"

"Sure, let's go to the offices first, though." Oliver winced. Jorja's enthusiasm was irritating him. He wasn't usually like this; today was really getting to him.

Jorja was enjoying her day out, Oliver could tell. He was happy that she was so easy to keep entertained because he was not in the mood to extend himself.

He could hear Josiah on the office phone when he entered the building. His door was open and he was squeezing a stress ball.

He hung up the phone when they approached and grinned.

"Good morning, Oliver. If you are here for work you are late."

"No." Oliver put down his laptop in an empty chair, "I am here to confirm that I am going to start working next week Monday. I need a one-week break from school and work."

"'Kay," Josiah said, "suit yourself. Last year you were a real asset to us so I can safely say that Dad will agree to those terms now." He looked over at Jorja and smiled. "Hello, Jorja Dennison. Are you looking for a job too?"

"No." Jorja shook her head. "Well, I wasn't, but if you have one..."

Josiah squeezed his stress ball. "There is always work on this farm, Cassandra our regular cashier, is off for six weeks. You could be our cashier. Oliver can teach you how to use the cash register and where everything is located."

Oliver grimaced. "That's work."

Josiah ignored him. "Unfortunately—or fortunately, depending on how you look at it, Jorja, you would have to start this Wednesday."

Jorja nodded eagerly. "Of course."

"Dress code is jeans and white tees," Josiah added. "Pay is weekly." He named a sum that had Jorja gasping. She hadn't expected so much.

"Okay then," Josiah looked at Oliver. "You look odd."

Oliver grimaced. "I am okay." He changed the topic hurriedly. "Jorja wants to see the greenhouses."

Josiah threw him a doubtful stare and then turned to Jorja.

"Sure, I can get Louis to show you around. He is our foreman." Josiah got up. "Let me introduce you to him. He'll get you up to speed on this place very quickly. You," he looked at Oliver, "stay put. I want to talk to you."

He left with Jorja and Oliver sank down in a chair. Josiah

was onto him; he must look like he felt—slightly dazed and somewhat fearful of his own thoughts. He was not sure that he could tell Josiah anything just yet, even though they had an easy rapport and were good friends.

Josiah was probably one of the secret-keeping sect. He never told anyone why he came from Kingston so suddenly.

Everyone around him was full of secrets. It made him feel suddenly lonely and distrustful of everyone, including his own mother. He felt like Truman in the movie the Truman show, where everybody around Truman knew that they were in a reality television show except Truman. Maybe everybody in Primrose Hill knew that something was off about his paternity except him and if Regina hadn't said something it probably wouldn't have dawned on him.

His name was Oliver Truman. No, Oliver Coke. Or was it? He sighed heavily.

He didn't even register that Josiah had songs playing on his computer till he heard the line of Sam Cook's song, *It's been a long, a long time coming, But I know a change gon' come, oh yes it will.*

He sat up straighter in his chair. He wished he could turn off the song but he didn't dare touch Josiah's computer. He usually acted strange when anybody touched his stuff.

Indeed a change was going to come in Primrose Hill, even if he didn't want it. Regina was like the cat among the pigeons and he was almost sure that her presence here was going to create quite a catastrophe unless she got what she wanted.

He jumped when a hand landed on his shoulder.

When he looked up he saw that it was Nolan Ramsey, the young pastor. He didn't look as if he was much older than Oliver. When they introduced him at church Oliver had marveled at how young he looked. He couldn't be more than twenty-one at the most.

"You were out of it, man," Nolan said pleasantly. "I was calling but you didn't hear."

"Yes, er, yes." Oliver nodded. "Sorry."

Nolan held up a large transparent bag of mixed lettuce, purple and green. "Josiah sent me in here to cash this."

"Oh yes." Oliver got up. "I'll do it."

"I was very happy to get this vegetable mix," Nolan said. "It seems as if this drought is driving a whole lot of business to this farm."

"Yes it is," Oliver said absently. "They are usually busy but the drought is actually profitable for hydroponics farmers."

"You are Nurse Allen's son?" Nolan asked, looking at him in concern.

Oliver nodded. "The one and only Oliver Allen at your service."

"Well, pleased to meet you, man. I am Nolan Ramsey."

"I know. Heard your sermon last week." Oliver weighed the lettuce on the side scale. "It was good. About casting lots in the Bible and the difference between that and palm readers, obeah or tarot cards and those sorts of things."

Nolan grimaced. "I may have stepped on some toes. I heard that a few persons up here still like to read their horoscopes and visit... erm... people who can read their future in tea leaves."

Oliver cashed the lettuce and handed Nolan his change. "There are usually a handful of those people in every country church and maybe town churches too, but I got your point. God allowed the Israelites to cast lots in order to determine His will for a given situation."

Nolan looked at him contemplatively. "You were listening."

Oliver nodded. "Don't be too impressed. I remember things exactly as they are said. I never have to take notes.

It's a gift and a curse."

"It's a gift. All good things come from God." Nolan smiled. "It made my day, hearing that a young man listened and remembered my sermon, even if he has that particular gift. There is hope for this country yet with you in it."

Oliver laughed, "Thank you, but you are not much older than me…you calling me young man feels odd."

Nolan nodded, "I am twenty-two."

"And this is your first church district, I reckon?" Oliver leaned on the counter interestedly.

"Yes it is." Nolan nodded.

"What did you do to the church heads that they would send you out here in the sticks?"

Nolan laughed. "Primrose Hill is not that bad. It's great actually. Good clean air, friendly people and working with a seasoned pastor like Pastor Ruel. I hope to learn a lot from him."

Oliver remembered once more that the people that he knew, including pastor Ruel, were probably knee deep in various secrets. He looked at Nolan Ramsey with his fair skin and round babyish face; maybe he could trust him with some of what he was thinking.

"You don't have any secrets, do you?" Oliver found himself asking before he could take it back.

Nolan raised his eyebrows. "Not that I know of. Wait," Nolan grimaced, "I was kicked out of college for non-payment of funds but God opened a way for me and I got back in. At the time I was so ashamed of being asked to leave and I kept it from everybody. What about you, have any secrets?"

Oliver swallowed. He wished he could say it. He wished he could just blurt it out. He wished that he had the guts but once it was out there it couldn't be taken back. Josiah came in just when he opened his mouth to take the plunge.

"Hey Oliver, sorry I took so long. A customer just came in with a big order. You can stay at the cashier desk?"

"Yes." Oliver sighed. "Sure."

"Maybe we can talk some more." Nolan was looking at him, a little concerned. "I am living two houses from Pastor Ruel. You know where that is?"

"Sure. Yes." Oliver nodded.

"Good." Nolan picked up his lettuce and walked out. Oliver knew he wouldn't approach him. The few seconds of insanity that had just gripped him had loosened its icy grip.

He would eventually get over this need to know the truth about his paternity, and he would pretend that he wasn't privy to all the other things that were swirling around in the community. He would pretend that everything was normal.

Chapter Eight

Ashley got up on Wednesday morning and contemplated not to go running. Maybe she wouldn't even leave the house today. She didn't want to meet up with Regina, who for the past three nights was coming to Bible study as calm as you please and even participating.

She was asking questions and acting as if she was some eager Bible student. Ashley had avoided going out for the past two mornings because of her but now she felt lousy. She needed to get rid of her pent-up energy.

She put on her clothes and looked over at Ruel who was as usual fast asleep. She went sleepily to the kitchen and was shocked to see Jorja dressed in jeans and white t-shirt eating cereal and watching television.

"Good morning," Ashley said politely. She reached into her cupboard for her water bottle.

"Good morning," Jorja said. her voice lacked resentment. "I am going to work today at the Rose Hill farms."

"Oh." Ashley was surprised. "I didn't know you got a job there."

"I did," Jorja said a hint of excitement in her voice. "It was a spur of the moment thing. Dad said I could take it."

"Good for you." Ashley was pleasantly surprised and slightly relieved. She wouldn't have Jorja underfoot all summer.

"I start work at seven and end at three," Jorja continued. "This evening I'll be home late. The Kincaids are throwing a birthday party for Jack."

"Oh yes." Ashley grimaced. "I was invited... really can't make it."

Jorja chuckled. "I was thinking of saying the same thing but Oliver convinced me to go. "

"Oliver Allen, huh?" Ashley grinned at Jorja. "He's a cutie."

"I know," Jorja giggled. "I really like him."

Ashley smiled to herself. Jorja was actually talking to her without the sulky resentment she had come to expect—what a miracle.

"He told me that you were nice and that I should give you a chance," Jorja admitted when Ashley spun around after rummaging in the cupboard for the bottle and finally finding it.

"God bless him," Ashley said simply. "Thank you for giving me a chance, Jorja."

Jorja put down her spoon in the bowl and then shook her head. "It was just the shock of it, you know, the changes. Mom died and then Dad married you and left..."

Ashley unscrewed her water bottle and took a sip.

"It's not even that Mom and Dad were so great together either. I guess even though they were not happy together I still wanted my family to be together."

Ashley almost choked on the water. She coughed and inhaled, trying to get her breath back.

"What do you mean not happy together?" Ashley wheezed out the last question while Jorja looked at her with concern.

"Didn't Dad tell you?" Jorja frowned. "He must have told you about him and Mom."

"He did," Ashley wheezed. "Said you guys were the perfect family. You went on missionary trips together, you had family devotions twice per day, you sang in a group called the Dennisons."

Jorja laughed. "Well...I wouldn't call us the perfect family... missionary trips were Dad's idea, because, well, my Mom would cause trouble and Mom hated the missionary trips. I hated them too. I just wanted to be in one place, making friends, being stable.

"Family devotions were torture because both my parents took to praying against each other so that the other could hear, Dad would say, 'Lord, please fix Rosalie's temper' and Mom would say, 'Lord, please allow Ruel to see that he is not a romantic husband.' I began to realize what they were doing when I was twelve. They were crazy, I tell you."

Ashley felt as if she were rooted to the spot. "But..."

"Oh, and as for the Dennisons, it was a pain singing with my parents. Our practice sessions would always end in a cold war with both of them arguing. They argued over everything and nothing and Mom would get real angry and throw things or...well let's just say that group was short-lived."

Jorja got up. "I guess I need to acknowledge the fact that Dad is so much happier with you. He has never been this content. I have to go brush my teeth."

"Okay," Ashley nodded, "I, er, I am going for my run."

Ashley stumbled out of the kitchen, leaving the water bottle behind on the counter. She couldn't even get her legs to run. She was concentrating on putting them one before the other as she walked through the gate. She couldn't wrap her mind around the fact that Ruel had blatantly lied to her.

He had told her some real whoppers about his former wife and life. He had listened to her lay out all her shortcomings about her previous marriage and had had the temerity to give her advice because he had come from such a loving and giving relationship. And now to find out that he hadn't been happy at all. Why lie to her though? Ruel didn't lie. He was as honest as they come.

The thought that she might not know Ruel as well as she thought did put a damper on her day. She honestly thought they were soul mates. In her mind Ruel had a Jesus attitude. She had always seen him in the light of a non-judgmental, accepting person, like Jesus was when the men brought the woman before him to be stoned.

"Ashley!"

She spun around and saw Josiah jogging toward her.

"Hey, you're out late this morning." Ashley forced a smile. Usually when she was going out Josiah was coming in.

"Yes, rough night," Josiah said, slowing down to talk to her. "One of our filters in a major fish pond stopped working… had to stay up until the guys fixed it."

"But now it's okay?" Ashley asked. She knew how seriously Josiah took his farming.

"Yes and ready to go." Josiah slowed to a walk. "You're feeling sluggish this morning?"

"Yes, kind of," Ashley nodded, "haven't jogged in two days."

"However did you cope?" Josiah laughed. "I have to exercise every single day or else I would go crazy. I exercise even when I am sick. When I was in Kingston I used to exercise with a premier league football team."

"That sounds grueling and fun. I used to do Pilates."

"It shows." Josiah glanced at her and then back at the road, a small grin on his mouth, "I went to one class at the gym and I didn't realize it was so challenging."

Ashley nodded. "Yes, it is challenging, I put in years of hard work--can't let it go to waste now."

"Do you miss it?" Josiah asked, inhaling the air loudly.

"It what?" Ashley stopped and stretched.

"Kingston," Josiah said, "the life there, the energy."

Ashley felt a flash of whimsy. She hadn't felt that way since she met Ruel and married him. Back then she was sure that she was doing the absolutely right thing. This morning's revelation by Jorja was working on her mind, though, because for the first time she felt a tiny lingering disquiet in her head about her husband.

"To be honest," Ashley straightened up from her long stretch, "I miss my apartment. I usually don't miss anything from my past but today you caught me feeling nostalgic. I bought it a couple years ago and I really did go all out in fixing it up. It's in a lovely location, pretty close to where I used to live. I like the convenient locations to supermarkets and clothing stores.

"And of course I miss my kids coming over occasionally. Now I hardly see them. Haven't seen them in months. I live too far into the hills here to expect anything different. Like this summer I could have them over pretty frequently if I was in Kingston; instead, I probably won't see them at all unless I go to Kingston. Before I go I would have to tell my husband and his wife...I mean ex-husband," she corrected herself quickly when Josiah raised his eyebrows."I have to tell him days in advance about me coming, so that I don't interrupt their schedule." She sighed. "Now you've got me going."

And she hadn't even realized how bitter she was feeling about the current arrangement. Maybe because Ruel had convinced her that she was supposed to be happy for whatever crumbs were doled out to her by Brandon and Nadine.

And she was feeling like so much of a sinner that she hadn't wanted to ask for more and Ruel had encouraged her to be content with what she had because she was the one at fault. But they were her kids. Hers!

For the first time in years Ashley felt militant and angry. What on earth was she doing for the past four years, sleeping? Allowing herself to become some kind of doormat because she had sinned?

And for the last year while married to Ruel, it was pathetic how much she tried to emulate his perfect first wife, and live the kind of life she thought he had before. And now this morning she was finding out it had all been a lie. There was no perfect life.

Talk about a wakeup call. This was hers.

"Sorry to get you going." Josiah started walking backwards so that he could better see her face. "I miss living in Kingston sometimes too."

Ashley looked at him fully; she didn't even remember what they were talking about initially. "Yes, Kingston. Why did you leave?"

Josiah stopped walking backwards and then turned around. "It's a long story."

"Can't be longer than mine." Ashley threw caution to the winds. She was feeling reckless. The shell of shame and secrecy that she had cocooned herself in all these years to keep up appearances was somehow weaker this morning and she found that she didn't care right now who knew about her past mistakes.

She looked at Josiah, his cleanly shaven face, his open and

ready smile, and decided that she would shock him.

"Five years ago my husband caught me in bed with another woman, I cheated on him before that with two other men and passed the children off as his. I got married to Ruel six weeks after meeting him, mainly because he was so understanding and sympathetic to my whole sordid story. Maybe I wanted someone just like that who could release me from blaming myself over the mess I made of my life. Who knows? Anyway, I moved here with him and that's why I am here."

Josiah's mouth was hanging open by the time she finished speaking.

"Your turn," Ashley said. "Just do it fast. It comes out easier then."

Josiah closed his mouth and then swallowed. "Well, you, er, had quite a time of it, didn't you?"

"You could say that." Ashley shrugged. "I am not blameless and I just realized this morning that that is okay. The important thing is that I am no longer like the Ashley of old. The thing is, instead of growing to be confident with the assurance that I am forgiven by God and Brandon, I have grown pathetic since then. I thought that I should just curl up in a ball and hide myself because I did wrong. Like I am the only person to have sinned. Yes, I have been pathetic."

Josiah nodded. "Everybody has something..."

"That's what Regina said." Ashley sighed. "She even said my stuff was not even the worst secret up here."

Josiah looked at her sharply. "What?"

"Your story." Ashley pointed at him. "You are not getting out of it that easily. I told you mine, you tell me yours."

"Fair enough," Josiah grimaced. "I worked at Prism Financials, a medium-sized accounting firm. I got the job because the interviewer thought I was cute."

Ashley chuckled.

Josiah pushed his hand in his pockets and then shrugged. "I guess mine is the anti-Joseph story. You know, when Potiphar's wife tried to entice him to sleep with her and he fled, preferring prison over sinning against God.

"Well, the interviewer was my immediate boss and to be fair, I did get the sensation that she was coming on to me from the day of the interview but I was so desperate to not come back to Primrose Hill and farming with my dad that I shrugged it off.

"Once I started working there, she hounded me for sex. I know it sounds ridiculous because it's usually the other way around, right?"

"I know there are women like that," Ashley murmured. "Trust me, I know."

Joseph coughed. "Oh yes, that, you dated women. Can we talk some more about your story? You know, I wouldn't have expected you to..."

"Your story," Ashley pointed at him. "And I didn't date women."

"Okay, okay, my story," Josiah sighed. "She bought me gifts, she made sure that I worked late with her and found opportunities to touch me. Honestly, it wasn't hard not to give in to her. I wasn't attracted to her, really. For one, she was married, and two, she was way older—I mean way older, like thirty years older, and I don't have mommy fantasies, and three, she was trying too hard.

"But one day, she announced to us at staff meeting that she would be laying off some persons from the department and she looked at me meaningfully across the table. I knew what that meant, play nice or else you are gone."

Josiah sighed. "I gave in. I became the boss' pet. For two whole years at her beck and call. I got several pay raises; she even bought me a car. You know, one of those high end ones.

"And I convinced myself it was okay to do it. I was a man; it wasn't the same as a woman, you know. I stopped going to church because let's face it, every sermon felt like a rebuke and I thought that people were judging me. And then, one night I was listening to the radio, something that I rarely do. I was half asleep, you know, drifting in and out of consciousness and I heard the announcer on the program say as clear as day, Josiah Coke, get out of that relationship."

"Are you serious?" Ashley widened her eyes.

"Yup," Josiah said, "I jumped up out of bed and started pacing. I listened keenly to the announcer again but he was not talking about anything to do with Josiah or Coke or relationships. They were discussing horse racing. It was then that I realized that it was God that spoke to me, so I got down on my knees and begged his forgiveness. Next day I broke off the relationship and she accused me of sexually harassing her and then fired me.

"There would be no recommendation from that company so I came home. It didn't make sense that I stayed in Kingston jobless when my dad needed the help here in Primrose Hill."

Ashley nodded and they walked together in companionable silence.

"Is that why Regina is up here?" Josiah finally asked. "Because of you?"

"Unfortunately." Ashley shrugged. "She is relentless."

"Does Ruel know about her?"

"Oh yes, I told him everything before we got married," Ashley said. "Have any suggestions on how to get her to leave?"

Josiah shook his head. "Point her to Jesus? Maybe she is up here for a reason; maybe it is her time to be saved."

"She's a cynic," Ashley murmured. "She doesn't believe in Jesus or God or any deity."

"She loves Bible study, though. Maybe she is losing some of that cynicism," Josiah said. "Maybe she has changed."

"She loves trouble and that is why she comes to the Bible studies," Ashley sneered. "I wouldn't put it past her to be planning something sinister right now as we speak."

*****

Regina woke up late again. She had slept fitfully the night before and when she had finally dozed off in the early hours of the morning she missed hearing the alarm clock or the fact that Lyn had let herself into the house and was now humming as she cleaned.

She hauled herself out of bed, washed her face and looked blearily into the mirror. Her eyes were swollen and bloodshot. Her cheeks and chin were rough and red where a long red rash snaked its way up from her neck. Her whole body was itching.

She ran for her bag and her Benadryl. She was allergic to something. Maybe it was something that she ate last night. She had gotten up in the middle of the night and gotten a pack of biscuits from Lyn's stash. Maybe it had in peanuts in there. She was severely allergic to peanuts and she had skillfully avoided contact with the nut through most of her life. Most packaged goods put a warning on their label about processing nuts. The biscuit she had had must have come in contact with nuts.

She staggered out to the living room and flung herself onto the settee. "Argh, I hate this."

Lyn stopped mopping the floor and looked up. "Wow, you look awful."

"It'll soon pass. It is not a bad bout, obviously, since I am still standing here. I took my Benadryl. It may be my peanut allergy."

"Mmm," Lyn murmured. "My daughter had a fish allergy. I mean it couldn't even touch her skin, but we prayed about it and God healed her."

Regina scratched her arms frantically. "Really now?"

"Yes," Lyn nodded. "If you are interested in healing you could ask them at the church to pray for you tonight."

"No thanks." She leaned her head back on the settee, wriggling her back to scratch against the settee's material. "I don't think God will answer any prayers with Norma Kincaid in their midst."

Lyn chuckled and went back to her mopping. "Maybe you are right."

Regina groaned. "Tell me something."

Lyn looked up. "Yes."

"How did the Kincaids make their money?"

Lyn paused. "Owen Kincaid's father owned quite a bit of the land around here and he had a dairy farm but it burnt down...they went into citrus farming after that."

Lyn stopped mopping altogether and leaned on the mop. "And then they sold some of the lands around this section of the hill because the old man needed the money. They used to live beside my family, you know," Lyn said contemplatively. "We didn't think they were rich then, really, they just had land. And then Owen married Norma. They had one of those back yard receptions, where they killed a goat and everybody came by for the meal. They weren't as fancy and had all of the airs they have now.

"I tell you, that Norma, even though I can't stand her, she is a hard worker. She used to have a stall in May Pen near the market. She'd buy and sell goods from Panama."

"Uh huh." Regina nodded.

"They couldn't afford a car to and from the market so they

used to push a cart—you know, those long wooden things with four wheels and a steering. "

"Oh yes," Regina said.

"They had to leave out before four o'clock each morning to reach May Pen by six-thirty. And I used to help out with babysitting—the eldest girl, Blossom, and then the second one, Sheryl. I babysat them with my own kids, free of cost too, because we were all hustling to survive and I understood.

"It's a pity they can't understand that I needed to sell those oranges that I took the other day because my youngest daughter Renee needs to pay her school fee. They even took away the job that I needed to survive. Wicked people. I guess they have forgotten what it's like to hustle."

"Hmmm." Regina murmured. "So how is it that they got so rich now?"

"After a couple of years Norma made it big with her buying and selling. She was very popular and then she opened a store and then they expanded. And then they started their employment agency business and it took off. They find jobs for people even in the States. I would have asked them to find one for me but of course I worked for them. I couldn't admit to them that I absolutely hated the pay and needed more, could I?"

"Impressive." Regina watched as Lyn resumed her mopping.

"Yes, impressive," Lyn said softly. "Some people have all the luck. Maybe if I had done some of that I wouldn't be where I am now—fifty-two, broke and still working as domestic help."

"You call it luck, I call it a good story. All I can say is that Owen and Norma Kincaid have a good cover for how they really got rich."

"Huh?" Lyn looked up at her sharply. "I always suspected

them. What do you know about them?"

"I know everything, dear Lynette," Regina started scratching her hair, "and I am seriously thinking that I am going to expose those two, but all in good time. You'll love it when I do."

Chapter Nine

"**H**ave you ever lied to me?" Ashley ran into the yard after her jog with Josiah, who was a million times fitter than she ever would be.

He had pushed her running up Mango Hill and when she had reached the top he had not even broken a sweat nor was he panting. He had turned off to go to his home and she had continued walking alone, remembering her conversation with Jorja about Ruel, and she was steaming by the time she reached home and saw him on the veranda, robe on and cup in hand.

He was looking at her now as if she had lost her mind, but she was not having any of that.

"Answer me," Ashley insisted.

Ruel put the mug on the wall and leaned back in his chair. "So you saw Regina again this morning and she cooked up some story to tell you."

"No," Ashley panted, "I did not see Regina this morning."

Ruel narrowed his eyes and looked at her. "Then why this ridiculous question?"

"Answer it." Ashley took off her sneakers one after the other and slapped them on the walkway. "Now."

"Is there something specific that I have done?" Ruel asked again.

"Yes. You told me that you had this perfect fairytale marriage before this and it was all a lie. Jorja told me this morning that you and your first wife didn't even get along."

Ruel sighed loudly. "Ashley, come on, I didn't want to mope around about the past."

"No, you didn't. Instead you wanted to fabricate it." Ashley huffed. "I don't know you, do I?"

"Come on, Ash. This is like the pot calling the kettle black. You lied to your first husband for years because of bad things you did. I just made my past seem a little more palatable than it was. Cut me some slack here."

"See, this is ridiculous." Ashley inhaled and then exhaled in a whoosh. "That was a different situation, and if there is one thing that I know, it is that once a liar it is hard to change. I lived a lie for years and I started this marriage thinking that I was actually in an honest relationship. I laid it all out for you, I told you everything about me and instead of being honest too, you gave me some cotton candy and fairytale story. You have just lost my blind trust, mister."

"Ashley come on," Ruel pleaded, "don't you think you are blowing this out of proportion?"

"No," Ashley pointed her finger at him, "because now I am going to wonder what else have you lied to me about and what you aren't telling me."

"You are being paranoid."

"Am I?" Ashley looked at him hard. "Am I really? Have you spoken to Regina yet?"

"No." Ruel sighed, "I am working on that."

"What kind of secrets does she have on you?" Ashley asked, realizing that she had dismissed what Regina had said before about Ruel having secrets. At the time she had thought it ridiculous; now she wasn't so sure.

"I can't imagine what." Ruel shrugged, unconcerned.

Ashley grunted and headed inside. Unfortunately, she didn't believe him. The first cracks were appearing in her marriage that she had thought was rock solid.

*****

Three days after his confrontation with Ashley, Ruel turned into the church's parking lot. Today was vestry day, where the members of the church could find him in his office. This was when they usually carried their documents for him to sign or came to request prayers or counseling.

He had promised to meet Nolan at the church office at nine so that they could run through the itinerary for the coming month but he was feeling a small fissure of fear for his marriage. Things were uneasy between him and Ashley.

The feeling had started when Ashley had come from her run a few mornings ago and announced that Regina had secrets on everybody, including him. The feeling hadn't completely left him since then and he felt as if he was on a chopping block and any minute now the guillotine would fall on his neck.

Coming clean to Ashley was not an option; coming clean to the church was a definite no-no. He would lose his job. A job which he still loved very much.

When he had said to Ashley that it was better if you didn't do something wrong in the first place so you wouldn't have anything to worry about, he was talking about himself.

In the past he had gone about things all wrong. Ashley had interpreted what he said differently, of course. He had long realized the danger of having Ashley put him on a pedestal but it had been a nice position to be in for a change. It had been nice to have a submissive wife who loved him; he had reveled in it. But now he realized that it was all going to end.

From the moment his mother called him and told him that he needed to come and get Jorja, he had known that reality was about to intrude.

And it had. He couldn't even blame Jorja. If he had told her to keep her mouth shut about their past, she would have found it odd.

He had banked on her resentment for Ashley to at least offer him some buffer against that, but Jorja was by nature a friendly girl. And since yesterday she was over the moon happy about her new job and meeting new friends.

He parked beside Nolan's car and took a deep breath. There were several ways that this mess he had found himself in could play out. There was no need to panic just yet.

He picked up his briefcase from the back of the car. He had quite a few counseling sessions today after his meetings with Nolan.

And he had to find out from Regina Tharwick exactly what it was she thought she knew about him.

Nolan was sitting in the office when he got there. A Bible was opened on the desk.

"Hello Pastor." He looked up and beamed. "I was going to..."

"Hi Nolan," Ruel interrupted him and put down his briefcase and sat at his desk. "I have a packed day, so let's get to it."

Nolan looked at him and frowned. "Everything okay?"

"Fine." Ruel smiled slightly and then went back to his

schedule book. "You got the okay to marry people yet?"

"Yes." Nolan nodded, "I was planning to officiate for one of my college friends' wedding in September so I applied for it from last year."

"Good." Ruel grumbled, running through the schedule, "I have a couple of requests here for Sunday. I can't be at two places at the same time so you can relieve me of one of those appointments."

"Okay," Nolan said hesitantly. "Can I ask why you are looking so glum?"

Ruel looked up from the book and then shook his head. "No. I am fine."

"Pastor Ruel, I may be young but I might be able to help."

"I doubt you can in this instance." Ruel drummed his hand on the table and then looked down in his book. "Some things I just have to sort out for myself without help."

Nolan cleared his throat. "I was going to tell you earlier that Sister Lynette Skinner called me early this morning. She wants me to pray for her boss. She's a visitor—Regina Tharwick, I believe her name is."

Ruel's head snapped up so fast he wasn't sure that he hadn't broken something.

"What's wrong with her?" he asked eagerly. Too eagerly, because Nolan frowned and was looking at him with a confused expression in his eyes.

"She has a food allergy. She is obviously allergic to peanut and milk but something else is irritating her for days now. Sister Lynette said her daughter went through something similar and was helped by prayer."

"Oh." Ruel's hopes deflated. He was wishing that it was something more than that. Something to get her out of the district. He had hopes of getting his marriage back to a semblance of what it used to be when Regina wasn't around.

"Do you want to come along?" Nolan asked. "It's my first home visit in this district."

No, he didn't want to visit the one woman who might be able to expose him. Before he could answer, Norma Kincaid pushed her head through the doorway.

"Hello gentlemen. Pastor Ruel, I am just passing by. I have to cancel our meeting today."

"Oh." Ruel was disappointed. There was his excuse not to go and see Regina, out of the window.

"Well then, that frees you up to come with me," Nolan grinned. "It's like the Lord is working on the timing on this case."

Ruel groaned inwardly.

"Well then, I guess it is a good thing I stopped by then," Norma said. "Where are you going?"

"To visit Regina Tharwick." Ruel looked at her and raised his eyebrow.

Norma's hands tightened on the door. "Really. Why are you visiting her?"

"She's ailing from food allergies," Nolan said, "so we are going to pray for her..."

"Food allergies?" Norma was trying to be casual but even Nolan picked up on her tension. "What sort of food allergies?"

"She doesn't know." Nolan looked between Norma and Ruel. "It's curious how you two reacted when I mentioned her."

Ruel got up. "Well, she is an, er, visitor. We don't want her to be sick on our watch."

"Yes." Nolan nodded, still looking doubtful. "Right."

"Well," Norma forced a smile on her face, "maybe you should encourage her to visit a hospital, far away from here."

Ruel nodded. "Hear that, Pastor Nolan? Isn't that an

excellent suggestion?"

"Well, yes." Nolan looked confused. "Couldn't she just check Nurse Allen at the clinic?"

"No," Norma said eagerly, "it's obvious that this is not the place to be for her to remain healthy. Gently nudge her to a better environment—after you pray for her, of course."

"Of course." Nolan got up too but he was wondering why Norma Kincaid and pastor Ruel suddenly looked so happy after he mentioned that Regina Tharwick was sick. Especially Pastor Ruel, who had walked in this morning like a cloud was hanging over his head.

*****

"She's swollen and blotchy and doesn't look like herself." Regina heard Lyn itemizing her symptoms one by one to some visitor on the veranda. "I told her that I had my daughter prayed for and she was healed but she is not into that sort of thing but I can't sit back and watch her decline right before my face."

"Yes, you can and you will," Regina garbled. Her tongue was slightly swollen too, a recent development, and her words were not as clear at it should be.

She pulled herself up on the sofa, her fingers were normal this morning but now they were almost twice their regular size. She had gotten worse over the past three days. She had stopped eating all processed foods in an attempt to mitigate this abnormal reaction of hers but it had only gotten worse.

She widened her eyes as far as her swollen lids would go when she saw Ruel Dennison and the young pastor step into the house behind Lyn, who was wringing her hands as hard as she could.

"I don't want him here." Regina pointed at Ruel. Her

stupid voice was weak and didn't have the sort of conviction that it should. "He killed his wife. Don't let him kill me too."

Lyn sighed. "Apparently she is hallucinating too. Sorry, Pastor Nolan. She doesn't realize that you don't have a wife."

Ruel stiffened when he heard Regina and he stared at her, willing her to shut up.

"Not the young one." Regina's tongue was heavy and it sounded like she said natheyounun.

Lyn looked at her in pity.

"Ruel the cruel." Regina tried again to put her point across.

Lyn sighed, "Regina just accept the prayers and get some relief."

"No prayers from murderers," Regina said, inhaling breathily. "No prayers from him."

Nolan moved closer to Ruel. "Sis Ashley is fine, isn't she?"

"Of course," Ruel murmured back. "When I left home she was very much alive. Regina looks terrible. She is swelling up right before our very eyes. We have to get her to the clinic."

Lyn overheard them and looked back. "You are right, pastor. Let me grab my bag."

She headed for the closet in the hallway.

"I'll call Honey," Ruel said, "and tell her what's happening."

"Everybody up here has secrets," Regina said. Her eyes were now swollen in a slit. "I remember where I heard the name Nolan Ramsey from."

"Shush Regina." Lyn got her bag and helped her from the settee. Nolan moved to her left to help her up.

"You. Nolan Ramsey. Shot your brother when you were younger. You were playing with your father's gun. Did he die?"

Nolan put her hands around his shoulders and sighed. "My father never owned a gun. I don't have any brothers."

"Yes, you do." Regina's voice was slurring even worse than before. "You are just like the rest of them up here. You're a liar. Norma Kincaid liar. Owen Kincaid liar. Ruel Dennison liar. Honey Allen liar."

They put her half-slumping body in the back of Ruel's car and Nolan and Lyn got in, propping her up between them.

"Okay." Ruel started the car and chuckled. "If I didn't see how swollen she is and the red rashes I'd say she was drunk."

Lyn nodded. "Maybe she is. She has these little bottles of vodka lined up in her room. They are all empty."

"It eases the pain," Regina slurred. "Ruel stole my Ash from me."

Nolan sighed. "I hope the clinic can also help her to come to her senses."

"You know, she is right about your name," Lyn said after a short silence. "There was a little boy that shot his brother named Ramsey, I can't remember if his first name was Nolan. It was all over the news a couple years ago. The father was a police inspector or something like that."

"Wasn't me," Nolan said. "As I said, no brothers or sisters and I never lived with either of my parents. I lived with my grandmother for most of my life until college."

"Oh." Lyn sighed. "Well then..."

"She jumps to conclusions a lot, doesn't she?" Nolan asked grimly. "She assumes that there is a conspiracy everywhere."

"I don't know," Lyn murmured.

"She just called Pastor Ruel a murderer," Nolan sputtered. "And all the other persons on our church board—she called them liars. Sick or not, that is unacceptable."

"He is a murderer and they are all liars," Regina muttered. "I have the proof."

She then slumped down, struggling to breathe.

Ruel sighed. "Ashley is quite fine. You will see her in

church tomorrow, hale and hearty. I am no murderer."

Regina roused herself from her crouched slumber to murmur, "Liar. All of them liars!"

*****

It was a slower than usual morning at the clinic for Honey. It was usually so at this time of the year when school was out and most of the small population of Primrose Hill citizens were gone on vacation elsewhere.

When she got the call from Ruel she was more than ready to receive Regina. The clinic boasted a complement of three nurses, with her included, and a few doctors who were rostered for one day per week. They always had a doctor in-house from nine in the morning to four in the evening. Today it was Dr. Ying. She was the doctor in residence.

She told Honey to knock on her door when the patient arrived.

Honey had no problem with that. She felt nervy this morning, though. She was almost twitching with it. She went to her office and glanced at her cell phone periodically, picking it up and putting it down.

Conroy had told her last night after the Bible study had finished that she needed to give him an answer today re his proposal or he would not be asking again. He had been proposing on and off for the past seven years, since they had both moved back to Primrose Hill. He wanted her to find her husband and get a divorce, so that she could move on with her life. Easier said than done.

She picked up the phone and then put it down.

"Lord, I am in trouble," she mumbled to herself feverishly. "I am in deep trouble. Deep, deep trouble. I should marry Conroy, it's long overdue, but that means I would have to come clean to both him and Oliver."

She pictured Oliver if she ever told him the truth and her heart quaked. He was the most precious person in the world to her. If she lost him, her life wouldn't be worth living. Everything up to now was done for her darling son.

These past few days, though, he was acting strange. Really strange. She stopped thinking about her dilemma and thought about him. He was mumbling when he spoke to her and acting surly and unhappy. Very unlike the Oliver of the week before and if she wasn't so caught up in her drama with Conroy Coke she would have realized sooner that her son was not the same.

He started working with Conroy today and he had left the house without even telling her goodbye. She needed to focus on him before she thought about marriages or confessions or any of that stuff.

"Nurse Allen." One of the nursing assistants popped her head through the office door. "The patient is here. Her face looks almost purple and her tongue is swollen."

Honey pulled on her efficient nurse persona and went to greet them at the clinic door. She indicated for them to come to the outpatient office and then she got Dr. Ying.

"Inflated tongue," Dr. Ying said, looking into Regina's mouth. "Food allergies, you said?"

Regina nodded. Her eyes were swollen shut and her nose was puffy and distended. She was breathing shallowly.

Honey looked at her from across the room. She looked totally different from the woman who had walked by her house almost a week ago. Then she had looked almost attractive, with her low-cut spiky hair and her light brown skin.

Despite the hideous tattoos decorating her body she didn't look too bad. Today, though, she was an inflated version of herself. Her face looked like a swollen frog.

The doctor gave her an injection and told her rest.

"Call me when the swelling is down," Dr. Ying said, heading back to her office. "Her breathing has to be monitored."

Honey nodded and sat down across from Regina.

She glanced at her watch. She should take the rest of the day off after Regina was stabilized and call Conroy over and tell him everything.

Get it over and done with. They had been dancing around each other for years now. It was time she stopped dancing. He wouldn't be around forever.

But if she told him she would have to tell her son. And when she told her son, he'd lose respect for her.

She would lose all sense of moral authority when people found out. They'd know she was a liar. Everybody would know. And they would mock her for it. She couldn't hold her head up high again, at church, or at home, or around Oliver.

Thirty minutes passed and Honey attended to two patients, helping them with their paperwork. She spoke to Pastor Ruel and Nolan and Lyn Skinner, assuring them that Regina would be fine. When she went back into the room Regina was sitting up in the bed. Her swelling had gone down significantly but vestiges of the rash were still in evidence.

"This place is killing me." Regina's voice was low.

"Welcome back to the land of the living," Honey said brightly, stepping into the room.

Regina snorted. "You!"

"Yes me, the lady whose flowers you like down the hill."

Regina groaned. "Oliver's mother. He is a nice boy. Pity he has you for a mother."

"What?" Honey froze mid-step. She was advancing toward Regina and was completely unprepared for that charge.

"You don't know who his father is, do you?"

Honey opened her mouth and then closed it. The question slammed into her like a jab. "Pardon me?"

"Surely that is God's duty, not mine." Regina hopped from the bed and wriggled her fingers. "Almost back to normal. I am not sure that I should stay up here anymore. Y'all are toxic."

"The doctor said I should call when you are awake," Honey stammered.

"No thanks." Regina yawned and stretched. "I am going back to Kingston. I will get a doctor who is unbiased and not a part of your little soap opera up here. How much do I owe you for the injection?"

"Well, this is a free clinic," Honey said, "but you should stay and hear what the doctor has to say."

"Nah." Regina pulled on her slippers. "Word of advice for you, nurse. You should tell your son the truth about his parentage. He's a nice boy."

"I don't know what on earth you are talking about." Honey could barely get her mouth to form the words, and the righteous indignation she was hoping for fell flat.

Regina rubbed her eyes and swayed a little. "Stop lying. If it makes you feel better, you are not the only liar at your church. Your pastor is a liar, Norma Kincaid is a liar and who knows who else."

She stumped out of the room, leaving Honey to stare at the swinging door.

Chapter Ten

"**A**nd then she came into the clinic, her face looking like meat that has been battered, and as soon as she got better she got out…said she didn't trust us up here, the place was toxic and that she was going back home. All I have to say is good riddance."

Oliver listened as his mother held center court around her captive audience. She came by to take him shopping for school supplies in the afternoon but she was stuck in the front office recounting the same story for everyone who would listen.

Today, it was Owen Kincaid. He was waiting in the front office to take Jorja to piano classes in the town after work. Everybody thought it was a brilliant idea, but Oliver wasn't too sure about that.

There was something about Jorja and how flirty she was to the men around her that made him uncomfortable.

He had told her not to try it with him, but then she had

turned her attention to Josiah and Uncle Conroy and any man who had come through the front door of the office. He didn't know if anybody else was registering how inappropriate it was for her to be so friendly and touchy with men, but for the past four weeks since she started working at Rose Hill farms she was the opposite of appropriate.

She rarely spoke to him anymore.

He watched as she walked past the office Josiah had assigned him and into Conroy's. As usual she was in one of her tight white t-shirts that outlined her full, high breasts pretty well and tight blue jeans. It seemed as if she deliberately stuck out her pert butt to emphasize its proportions.

She had a new vampish walk that she adapted when she passed the office where he was stuck filing for the past couple of weeks. Josiah might be a genius at accounting but he sucked at secretarial work. He needed a secretary.

Jorja passed the office and flipped her braids over her shoulder, giving him one of her red-lipped pouts.

"Hey Oliver."

"Hey Jorja." He looked back down at the files in his hand and pretended that he hadn't been watching out for her.

He reminded himself that there were only two weeks left and Charlotte would come back. Nice, solid old Charlotte, who reminded him of his mother's grand-aunt Myrtle.

He had tried to talk to Josiah about Jorja and her over-sexualized appearance and actions but Josiah had misinterpreted his concern as him having some form of crush on her and being afraid to talk to her.

Ridiculous.

It was ridiculous. He wasn't afraid to talk to her, nor was he jealous. He didn't even like Jorja. At least he wasn't sure.

But how did one explain his sudden fascination with all that she did? So far this week he had caught her in Uncle

Conroy's office, her hand resting on his shoulder as they looked over a purchase order together.

Somehow the pose hadn't looked innocent to him and he had been filled with a kind of uneasiness that hadn't left him for the whole day, especially when Conroy had looked up at her, a softening in his eyes. It looked too intimate. Too wrong somehow.

And last week when Uncle Owen had come to pick her up he could have sworn that when he opened the door for her to precede him his hand had rested too close to her butt instead of her mid-back.

He was suspicious of every man she came into contact with, including his honorary uncles, who were pillars among the faithful Christian men.

He didn't like feeling this way, suspicious and distrustful of them, and he had Regina to thank for that.

Since the day that she had blurted out that everybody in the place had secrets, he had been hyperaware of everyone, including his own mother.

Regina changed him. She had torn off his rose-colored glasses and showed him that the world was not all innocent and hunky-dory; that was when he started watching Jorja.

He heard his mother's shoes clicking on the floor as she walked toward his office. She waved to him, a smile on her face.

"Hey you. What's going on? Ready for our afternoon date?"

"Yes." He nodded to her. "Let me just finish up here."

"I am going to say hi to Conroy." Her smile dimmed a bit. She and Conroy must have had some kind of fight or something because they were not on very friendly terms anymore.

It was nothing overt, just a hint of frost between them.

Conroy didn't come around for breakfast anymore and when they had lunch at the Kincaids' after church these days he was conspicuously absent.

He had tried to ask his mother about his father on about five occasions since Regina had planted doubts in his head but every time he did, his mother managed to change the subject.

And she didn't even do it well. He had allowed her to do it because he had a sense of panic that he wasn't going to like what he heard. But this evening he had made up his mind that she would tell him something on their drive to May Pen. They would have to talk; she would have no escape.

*****

They drove out after Owen Kincaid and Jorja. His mother's old Camry sputtered before it started.

And she cursed under her breath.

"I heard you." Oliver grinned at her. "You swore. Whatever will your Christian friends say, Sister Honey?"

"They would say I understand wholeheartedly, Honey, that your car would make a Christian curse. This car is acting up again." Honey sighed. She finally got it to start after several tries. "Maybe I should just take it to the garage when we get to May Pen and let George have a look at it."

"I don't think George knows much about what he is doing," Oliver muttered. "I can have a look at it."

"Nope." Honey smiled at him lovingly. "Those hands are doctor's hands. Designed to save the world. You will need them when you go to Africa for your mission trip.

"George is the only reason why this piece of junk is still on the road. Okay, let me see if I have the shopping list."

She rummaged in her bag and frowned, finally pulling out

a long piece of paper.

"Here it is!"

"What's going on between you and Uncle Conroy?" Oliver asked while she took the car out of park and drove through the gates.

"He asked me to marry him. I didn't give an answer by his ultimatum so he is giving me the cold shoulder." Honey glanced at Oliver.

"And you are already married too," Oliver pointed out. "Shouldn't you divorce one husband before you can get hitched to another?"

"There is that," Honey sighed, "and the fact that I am mulling over some job offers that will take me away from here. Once you are in university I just might take them up. I think Conroy is becoming fed up with me."

"You love him?" Oliver settled in the seat.

"Yes, no, I guess," Honey said contemplatively. "Sometimes I think that because we are both back here and basically putting down roots in this place, maybe I should settle down. I could do much worse than Conroy."

"Doesn't sound as if you are sure." Oliver adjusted his seat and glanced at his mother.

"I loved him when we were younger. Young love is always intense and crazy and idyllic. That brings me to the topic of Jorja. What's up with that girl?" Honey huffed, "I saw her in the office hanging over his shoulders. They were almost lip to lip."

Oliver glanced at his mother sharply. "You see it too?"

"Yup," Honey said. "Totally inappropriate. I am going to have a talk with that girl."

Oliver sighed. "You should and talk to Uncle Conroy too."

"Oh yes, I will. Hopefully he'll listen to me," Honey growled. "Touchy-feely teenage girls have gotten better men than him in trouble. She doesn't touch you and stuff, does she?"

"No. Come on, Mom." Oliver squirmed in his seat.

"You like her?"

"No. Not really. I don't know. She is growing on me, I guess." Oliver shrugged. "She is pretty."

"But she dresses like a slut. I should talk to her father too," Honey said harshly. "What's with all of that eye makeup? Makes her look like a clown."

"She doesn't look like a clown," Oliver defended Jorja. "You should find nicer things to say about people."

"Hmmm," Honey muttered.

"And you should stop talking about Regina and her allergies and how awful she looked. You sound so happy that she was sick. What kind of nurse are you?"

"She deserved it," Honey said promptly. "She had the most awful things to say about me and other people. And she thinks she is the so-called keeper of secrets. But God fixed her right; big bad Regina could barely see because God struck her with allergies."

Honey laughed again. "I hope she never comes back to Primrose Hill. I have a mild dislike for her and her big mouth."

"Am I Conroy Coke's son?" Oliver blurted out before he could stop it.

His mother sobered up and slowed down the car and then she started laughing again. "What a question! Where did that come from?"

"Just asking."

"Because of that Regina woman, I'd bet."

"Mom," Oliver sighed, "just answer!"

"No, you are not Conroy Coke's son."

"Honestly?" Oliver prompted. "You are not telling me

lies?"

"No lies," Honey said solemnly. "Conroy and I never did the dirty."

"Sex is not dirty," Oliver said, exasperation creeping in his voice.

"What do you know about it?" Honey glanced at him sternly.

"I am seventeen years old. I know quite a bit," Oliver said grumpily. "Don't change the subject."

"When you say know, you mean theory, right?" Honey asked nervously.

"Yes Mom." Oliver tensed up for the sex talk. His mother thought that telling him about diseases and pregnancies would scare him. "I don't want to talk about sex now, Mom."

"Well, who better to talk to?" Honey grumbled. "Your father is not around to give you a manly perspective; I have to give you all the info I know."

"Tell me about my dad," Oliver said quickly. "I just know his name and his profession. I really have no other information."

"Not this father talk again." Honey grimaced. "I'd rather not talk about that poor excuse for a man and..."

"And..." Oliver asked eagerly. His mother might be sulking but she was in the mood to talk.

She pushed back a hank of curly hair and then slowed down the car. "Isn't that Owen's vehicle?"

Oliver looked at it. It was a silver Lexus SUV. They couldn't see the license plate number. It was parked at the side of the road in a clutch of trees and was barely visible from the road. If his mother didn't have eagle eyes they wouldn't have seen it. The windows were dark. They couldn't see inside the vehicle from their vantage point, even if they wanted.

"Why is he parked?" Honey asked suspiciously.

Oliver sat up in the car seat and looked at his mother, his heart tripping like crazy. "Maybe he is talking on the phone."

Honey looked at him, doubt in her face. "If this car was reliable I would stop and see how long this phone call takes, but if I stop I might not be able to start again."

"You don't think it's him, do you?" Oliver was afraid to voice what he was thinking aloud.

"No," Honey murmured. "Not at all. Owen is more sensible than that."

*****

"Which tie should I wear?" Ruel held up three ties for Ashley to choose from. She was sitting in the living room with wrapping paper scattered around her. They were both going to Ariel's birthday party and they would stay in Kingston for two days.

Ashley looked up from the paper and shook her head. "It's casual dress, dear. She'll be seven. Her party will include other children her age. You'd be grossly overdressed."

"Yes, right." Ruel nodded and left the room.

"Clueless Dad." Jorja giggled in the corner of the settee, where she was ensconced with a novel. "Maybe if he had thrown a birthday party for me when I was growing up, he would know how to dress."

"You never had a party?" Ashley asked as she put the final touches on one of the gifts.

"Nope," Jorja snorted. "It was cool, I didn't want one anyway. I always preferred to hang out with the kids older than I was and Dad thought that I had inappropriate friends. Besides, there was Mom. She was a loose cannon. No one wanted their children around her."

"You did have inappropriate friends." Ruel came into the

room and sat on the settee above Ashley. He was ignoring the part about Rosalie. Ashley let it slide without comment.

"Are you sure you are okay with staying at the Kincaids for the two days while we are away?" Ruel asked Jorja.

"More than sure." Jorja picked up her book again. "Uncle Owen usually takes me to music class, so it is no problem just dropping me at his home instead of here. And Aunty Norma is over the moon happy to have me stay over. I will just stay out of Jack's way; you don't have to worry about me."

"Okay." Ruel turned on the television and reclined his seat. He turned to a news channel that was discussing human trafficking.

"Boring," Jorja said, looking over the top of her book. "If you are going to disturb the peace with boring stuff, maybe I should go to my room."

"This is serious business," Ruel said. "I was reading about some of the horror stories in the newspaper the other day. You know that human trafficking is big business for some of these so-called recruiters, who lure their victims with the sweet promise of jobs and other things and then they sell them all over the world for various atrocities, including selling their organs."

"Ugh." Jorja got up. "Sad and depressing. "Good night folks."

"Goodnight, Jorja." Ashley finished wrapping her presents while Ruel listened to his program.

"You realize how peaceful the days are since Regina left?" Ashley got up and sat beside Ruel. "It's like the air is cooler, the grass is greener and it rained twice."

Ruel chuckled. "And you've forgiven me for the unforgivable blunder of not being upfront with about my previous home life."

"Yes." Ashley snuggled up to him. "You promised that you'd never lie to me again, ever."

"That I did." A cloud passed over Ruel's face but he brushed it away by pulling Ashley even closer and burying his nose in her fragrant hair.

Chapter Eleven

Brandon and Nadine Blake lived in a fancy house overlooking Kingston. Ashley always felt odd coming by. In a deep, secret part of her she would always consider Brandon her husband.

And she hated it that she had allowed selfishness and restlessness and whatever it was that had driven her to hurt him over and over again to end their marriage. Sometimes she still couldn't believe that she had done all of those horrible things to Brandon. It was like she was another person then.

Every time she came by and saw him with his new family and saw how happy the girls were, it depressed her. She had nobody to blame for her situation but herself.

She gripped Ruel's hands tighter as they made their way up the picturesque walkway to the massive front door.

Her hands trembled on the gifts that she held and the thought once more assailed her that she was tired of being the Santa Claus in her children's lives. Before Ruel could knock on the door it was opened by Beatrice Blake, Brandon's mother. Still the warm, sweet person that Ashley had selfishly resented at one time in her life.

"Oh, Ashley and Ruel," Beatrice smiled at them. "Come on in. Welcome."

She stepped back and allowed them to step into the foyer. "I am going to get some stuff from my car. Nadine is around the kitchen area. Brandon is helping out by the pool."

Ashley nodded and headed to the kitchen, where Nadine was sitting at the breakfast nook decorating a giant cake shaped like a princess.

"Hey, you two." She smiled at them and looked genuinely happy to see them.

Ashley forced herself to smile lightly. She wasn't happy, though. She was experiencing pure and raw jealousy at the moment.

Nadine was living her life and she was pregnant again, barely showing, but there was the briefest glimpse of a bump and her skin was glowing.

She looked really contented.

"You can put the pressies outside, Ashley."

"I will." Ashley nodded and tried not to smile through gritted teeth. "I see congratulations are in order."

"Yes, yes. Thank you." Nadine looked down at her belly. "I am four months along."

"Mommy, can I not go to this children's party? I want to go to the movies with Tara."

Ashley swung around and her heart melted. It seemed as if in the last couple of months Alisha, her firstborn, had grown a couple of inches taller.

"Alisha," she whispered.

"Hi Ashley." Alisha smiled at her as if she was a pesky acquaintance, no greeting in her face, and then turned back to Nadine. "Can I just please for one minute be exempt from little children's things?"

Ashley's heart collapsed. She didn't know what to do. Her hands were trembling hard on the presents. Ruel took them from her.

"I'll just go and put these with the others and say hi to Brandon." Ruel excused himself and greeted Alisha politely. She barely glanced at him.

"Mommy, yes or no."

"Sit down," Nadine said to Alisha sternly. She was looking furious and Ashley wasn't sure if it was on her behalf.

Alisha sat down abruptly on one of the stools at the counter, and Ashley was left standing in the room.

Nadine stood up with the cake. "Now greet Ashley properly. And no, you are not going to the movies with Tara. Tara is going to be at this kiddy party too."

Alisha groaned and put her head in her hands.

Nadine left them both in the room and Ashley looked at Alisha and didn't know what to say. This young girl teetering on the edge of womanhood was her child and she had no idea what to say to her.

She felt like a stranger. And it hurt.

She pulled up a stool close to Alisha and swallowed. "So, how are you?"

"Good." Alisha held up her head and looked at her warily. "You are going to ask me about school and that sort of thing, aren't you?"

"Well," Ashley frowned, "I did speak to you on the phone last week and you told me you aced your exams."

Alisha smiled, with perfectly aligned teeth. Ashley felt as if she had bequeathed something worthy to her. She was searching for some connection to this first child of hers who just deliberately and pointedly made her feel excluded.

There was silence for a moment and then Alisha looked at her, "I am sorry for my behavior earlier."

"Apology accepted." Ashley's voice was hoarse and tear-filled. "I haven't seen you in a long while, can I get a hug?"

She held out her arms and when Alisha got up she got up too, and she clutched her firstborn to her so tightly she didn't know if she would let go.

"Sorry to break up this moment," Brandon said from the doorway, "but there is a little birthday girl who wants to say hi to her mother."

"Ashley!" Ariel ran towards her, joy lighting up her little face. "I missed you, Ashley."

"I missed you too, Ari," Ashley said, hugging her little girl to her, inhaling her scent.

"When are you coming back to live in Kingston?" Ariel asked. "It's not as much fun shopping with Mommy as it is with you."

Ashley laughed and wiped away the tears from her cheeks. "I don't know, kiddo."

"You should move back," Alisha piped in too. "Mommy said I am at the age where having two mothers is a plus."

Ashley chuckled. She heard Nadine coming back into the kitchen. "Thanks Nadine."

"It's the truth," Nadine said from behind her.

"We need to talk to Ashley for a while," Brandon said to the girls and they nodded.

When they left Brandon looked through the window. He was still so handsome. Maybe even more so, in his red shirt, which showed off his buffed arms and blue jeans, which highlighted that he had been working out.

"I have Ruel blowing balloons." He turned back to Ashley. "That should keep him occupied for a while."

"What do you want to drink?" Nadine asked, heading for

the fridge.

"You guys are making me feel anxious," Ashley said, looking from Brandon's concerned face to Nadine's. "I'll have orange juice if you have it, thanks."

"I do." Nadine poured the drink and carried the glass over to the nook. "Come on, sit down."

Ashley sat before her and Brandon. "Don't tell me that this is bad news."

"Well," Brandon frowned, "this is going to sound really odd."

He lowered his voice to almost a whisper. "Regina called me two days ago at the office. And she told me the oddest things about Ruel."

Ashley groaned. "What is she doing now? I can't be rid of this woman."

"Wait," Brandon furrowed his brow. "She is not just making trouble for you, Ashley, what she is saying is legit. Ruel Dennison went on vacation with his first wife Rosalie, they met in an accident and she died, while he did not receive a scratch. Their life up to that vacation was turbulent."

"Stop." Ashley held up her hands. "No, I don't want to hear this."

"Regina thinks that he murdered her. There is no record of any accident during that time in Florida state where they were. She also said that you would not listen and that she was concerned for you."

"Ashley, if you are in danger..." Nadine whispered, "you should get out."

"No, no, no, this is ridiculous." Ashley couldn't think with them looking all concerned and spouting madness about Ruel. "Regina is obsessed with me. She'll make up anything. Ruel is a good person."

Brandon and Nadine sighed and looked at each other.

"You be careful," Nadine finally said.

Chapter Twelve

"**Y**ou always look grim after a visit with the Blakes," Ruel said ruefully. "Maybe we should stop seeing them."

"Impossible," Ashley murmured, "they have my kids."

Ashley was feeling grim. She could not relax enough to enjoy the party and she had been reluctant to leave with Ruel—all sorts of thoughts were ricocheting in her head.

Chief among them was the fact that Regina had contacted Brandon. The irony of that was not lost on her. Regina hated Brandon and vice versa; for her to have contacted him was like a message in and of itself.

They entered her apartment and she looked around in the spacious apartment space and realized that she was missing the usual pleasure of coming back home. Right now she was feeling numb.

She sat on the settee heavily and kicked off her shoes.

Ruel sat in front of her. "This is worse than I thought. You are not talking at all. Actually, I thought the party went off pretty well. The..."

"It's not the Blakes this time. It's just..." Ashley bit her lips. "Tell me about Rosalie."

"Rosalie," Ruel groaned. "Ashley, please..."

"Tell me how you two met. What was your life like, exactly? Don't leave anything out. I especially want to know how she died."

Ruel closed his eyes and didn't move for such long time Ashley wondered if he fell asleep. Eventually his eyelids fluttered as if he was suppressing the movement.

"We met at a church camp. Her parents were abroad at an evangelistic crusade and she was too much of a handful for her grandmother. At the time I didn't know what handful meant. I just thought she was a little high-strung. We were both sixteen and Rosalie was cute. Her father was a pastor, and I wanted to be a pastor. It was perfect.

"Her parents died the final year of university and my feelings were kind of waning for Rosalie but she was on her own, and was an only child. She had no one so I married her. I didn't really see the cracks until we were married, though. She had hidden it so well and sometimes I wonder how she did it."

He paused.

Ashley leaned forward. "Go on."

"I have never spoken about this with anyone before," Ruel sighed, "except her doctors. She, ah...had issues, mental issues. One of them was intermittent explosive disorder. She would just suddenly go into violent rages. You've heard of road rage?"

"Yes," Ashley gasped.

"Well, something like that, and she had other issues but as the years went by she got more violent and..."

"What?" Ashley was now tense. Was he going to confess

that he subdued her and killed her for his own safety?

"And abusive. I tried to hide it from Jorja when she was growing up but she has seen her mother in various states of... er... agitation. It wasn't until a year and a half ago when Rosalie pulled a knife on Jorja for not washing the dishes that I realized that something had to be done. She was getting worse. She would hurt somebody if she wasn't stopped. So I arranged for a vacation."

"Oh God," Ashley put her head in her hands.

"And we met in that accident," Ruel finished weakly.

Ashley hung her head. She couldn't look at him. "Did you kill her?"

"No." Ruel sighed. "No. I did not. Ashley, look at me."

Ashley slowly held up her head. It felt heavier than her body.

"Do you seriously think that I could with a clean conscience lead God's people if I were a murderer?"

"I don't want to think so," Ashley whispered. "But I can't help but think that her death was too convenient and our meeting after that even more so."

Ruel sighed. "About that. I have always wanted to confess this to you."

"What?" Ashley stiffened again.

"I saw you before that convention. I saw you at your store. You were walking to your car. I was passing by and I stopped and watched you for a long time, while you moved something from your car and back again and I sat there and I wished that I was single and we could talk. I noticed that you had no ring on your finger. I even inquired about you and heard that you were a divorcee."

"Really? How long ago was this?" Ashley's heart was doing that weird tripping thing again when she was nervous.

"Two years ago." Ruel moved before her and held her

hands in his. "Ashley, I think we were meant to be together. I love you with all my heart. I can't imagine a day in my life without you in it."

Was this two years ago when he was planning to kill his wife? Ashley's hands trembled in his. And Ruel lifted them to his lips.

"You are so beautiful and kind and all mine." Ruel kissed his way up to her arms but Ashley wasn't feeling anything, really. He reached her lips and was breathing hard by the time Ashley registered what he was doing.

She pushed him away.

"Not tonight, Ruel. I have a million and one things on my mind right now."

She walked toward the room, a heavy, listless feeling in her stomach. Something was not right here. Something was definitely off.

*****

They went to pick up Jorja a day later. Ashley had spent the day before avoiding Ruel. She had picked up Ariel and Alisha and they had spent almost all day shopping. He had disappeared till late in the evening. He had also slept in the guest room and he was looking wounded, as if she had done something wrong to him.

As far as Ashley was concerned he should be happy that she was coming back with him to Primrose Hill. She was still not sure about his account of the Rosalie story and she was even further in doubt when Nadine had urged her to get the story straight before she became another dead wife.

Lord, this is not good, Ashley breathed under her breath and glanced at Ruel. He looked the same, tall handsome fine features; he smelled the same, Brut perfume; but he was not the same to her anymore. It was amazing how her emotions had been tied up in him when she had thought that he was perfect and good. Now she wasn't even sure that she loved him!

She now was looking on Ruel as her punishment for crimes past, not the redemption that she had expected him to be.

Had she really loved him or had she been grateful somebody, a man of the cloth, could hear her story and still want to marry her? But as she was finding out, there were no guarantees with men. She only had God to depend on.

Also, a little part of her was thinking that she deserved this, a flawed man; after all, she had thrown away her first marriage in a fit of selfishness, strung her husband along for years and literally broke him down.

Seeing Brandon happy and contented with Nadine and growing her children she had thought was torture, but this was her real punishment. She was with a potential wife killer. Maybe she was next, as Nadine had implied, and maybe she deserved it.

They drove up to the curving driveway of the Kincaids' house and were met at the front by Norma, who was not looking pleased. She was also uncharacteristically underdressed in a dress that looked stained and washed out, and her hair was in a loose bun.

She greeted them abruptly. "Ruel, Ashley. Sorry for my appearance; I was about to dye my hair."

Ashley smiled. She had never really given it thought that in order to maintain her jet-black hair Norma must have done something to it. After all, she was fifty.

"Listen," Norma said, "your girl, Jorja, is pregnant."

Ashley gasped and leaned on the car.

Ruel was looking at Norma as if she had two heads.

"Yup. Pregnant." Norma shook her head. "I caught her

chucking up her food this morning. I forced her to take a pregnancy test this afternoon and it was positive. She claims she is four weeks along."

Ruel hadn't spoken yet but his face was a picture of surprise. "Who could it...where is she?"

Norma pointed her thumb over her shoulder. "Downstairs packing. I asked her who was the father and she started crying. I don't know, maybe you can get it out of her. If I were you I would get in front of this. That is how you handle problems, slam them down before they can grow into bigger problems."

Norma was almost shaking with indignation. "Can I tell you how utterly embarrassing for you this will be, Ruel?"

"Yes," Ruel sighed, "I imagine it will be an embarrassment. People will wonder how can I lead the church when I can't rule my own house. I say find out who the father is and then get them married as soon as possible."

"Maybe we are jumping ahead here," Ashley said, trying to inject some sanity into the situation; she had never seen Norma so worked up. "We should talk to Jorja first, before we talk marriage and all of that."

Norma snorted. "When my girls were that age they didn't even know what sex was; now your girl, the pastor's kid, is doing it. Preposterous, I tell you."

Ruel sighed.

He looked totally trampled on, like he was at a loss as to what to do. Ashley's heart melted. She hated seeing him this confused but she didn't move to comfort him. Maybe Jorja's pregnancy was the least of his worries right now.

Chapter Thirteen

"**W**hose child is it, Jorja?" They were all sitting in the living room. Jorja had just finished a dramatic crying jag that Ashley suspected was not totally real. She was making sounds without looking remotely sorry.

Ruel was holding on to his temper by a thread. Ashley watched as he clenched his hands together and then unclenched them.

"I didn't even know that you were having sex. I stupidly thought that..." his voice trailed away. "You are going to tell me who this guy is, or you can't live here anymore."

"Ruel!" Ashley said, alarmed.

"That's just the way it is going to be," Ruel said harshly. He was livid. "She's old enough to get pregnant. She's old enough to live on her own."

"But Daddy!" Jorja started crying afresh. "I don't know who the father is. It could be anybody. I like men. I sleep with them. They tell me that I am pretty."

Ruel's face took on a crazed mask that made even Ashley afraid.

"Give me names," Ruel gritted out. "Names. Now."

Jorja seemed as if her whole body was trembling. "There is Oliver..."

Ashley closed her eyes and shook her head. Oliver Allen--she had expected more from him. Honey Allen was going to go crazy; he was her prized baby, her sheltered only son.

"Who else?" Ruel asked harshly.

"Conroy and Owen—oh and the guy I do music lessons with, Gary."

Ruel was frozen speechless.

Ashley had to intervene now though, before Ruel did something foolish. She was feeling as shell-shocked as he was. "Conroy Coke and Owen Kincaid…"

"Jorja, go to your room now," she said hoarsely. "Go now!"

Jorja scrambled up and almost ran to her room.

Ruel clutched his heart and then slumped in the sofa. "I can't process this...my daughter is a slut...this is my fault, all of this is my fault. I need to go…"

Ashley watched as he stumbled toward the study. She was left in the hall with a bemused expression on her face.

*****

Breakfast was a solemn affair, filled with tension. Ruel's eyes were red, it seemed as if he hadn't slept, and Jorja hunched over her cereal, looking as if someone had whipped her within an inch of her life.

Ashley was also feeling weary; she hadn't slept all that well last night either. She had been running through the names of the men who Jorja had said were potentially her baby's father. It just seemed bizarre.

The kitchen was silent except for the clanking of the spoons on the bowls. Ruel wiped his mouth and said to Jorja quietly, "I know you were lying last night just to make me mad. Now just be honest and tell me who it is that knocked you up."

Ashley almost smiled at the term that Ruel used. He must be off his game to be using words like 'knocked up'. She had never heard him talk like that before.

"Jorja!" He slammed his fist down on the table, which made both Ashley and Jorja jump. "You can't go around trying to destroy the reputations of these men. It is malicious. Now tell me, who is it that you had sex with? Was it Oliver Allen?"

Jorja nodded, her head almost down in her plate.

Ruel got up. "Well then, I am going to have a talk with Honey Allen today."

Jorja didn't move. She was still hunched over like a dog that had been kicked too many times and didn't have the energy to respond.

"Maybe I should go with you," Ashley suggested.

"Okay." Ruel wiped his hand over his face in a gesture of defeat. "I want to catch Honey before she leaves for work."

*****

Oliver was in the greenhouse when he heard the commotion at the front of the house. His mother was yelling "No! No! No!" at someone, like she had just heard devastating news.

He dropped the water can and ran around to the sound of her voice.

He was shocked to see Pastor Ruel and Sis Ashley in the front yard. Pastor Ruel didn't look so good. He looked ruffled. His tie was askew and Ashley looked troubled.

Her eyes connected with his and he read discomfiture and

disappointment. He wondered what he had done. He didn't have to wonder long.

His mother turned around and looked at him. She was quivering. Oliver knew what that meant. She was seriously angry. He ran through all of the things that he could have possibly done and he couldn't come up with anything. At least not anything that would involve the pastor and his wife.

"Oliver Nathan Allen." His mother spit out his full name. "Did you have sex with Jorja Dennison?"

Oliver froze. His eyes swung from his mother to the pastor and then to Ashley.

"No." His voice was weak when he said it and he could almost see the doubt flashing across his mother's face. "No!" He said it louder and stronger.

His mother staggered where she stood and she inhaled and then exhaled loudly.

"Well Pastor, you heard, my son is not a potential candidate for your daughter's paternity lottery. Maybe you should check Owen Kincaid or Conroy Coke."

Ruel looked at Ashley and then back at Honey. "What are you talking about?"

"I saw things," Honey said, "that have me drawing certain conclusions. I was even going to talk to you about your daughter's obvious and blatant flirtations with these men."

Honey looked at Ashley scornfully. "And you as female guardian—you let that young girl out of the house in the tightest of jeans and t-shirts. She was acting like a mini-whore around Conroy and we saw what looked to be Owen's vehicle parked at the side of the road, with her presumably in it!"

Jorja was pregnant. Oliver felt a tinge of disappointment and then incredulity; she had really slept with one of those old men.

He had felt dirty even thinking about the possibility of sleeping with Jorja when he had seen her flitting around the office and now here it was, a reality.

Pastor Ruel did not say a word. He walked back to the car, his back ramrod straight, like someone who was dealt the harshest blow and didn't know what to do. Oliver felt like going to offer some comfort but he doubted that that would be welcomed right now.

Ashley lingered though. She looked at Honey. "I am sorry about this. Jorja had a list of men that could have been her baby's father. Oliver's name was first."

Honey grunted. "Just don't drag my son's name into any of this mess. Don't include Oliver's name with that girl's. I mean it."

"I understand." Ashley looked at Oliver. "Sorry again."

Oliver nodded. "It's okay. I wonder why she said me, though; she hardly spoke to me these past couple of weeks."

"That's because she was busy doing other things with other people. She might be hiding the identity of the real father too." Honey snorted. "If it is Conroy's so help me, I'll kill him. As for Owen Kincaid, I am sure Norma would do the same. Do us all a favor, Ashley, and tell Pastor Ruel to be very sure before he goes hunting for the father."

Ashley nodded again and then looked over at the garden. "I seriously love those yellow flowers."

"They are daffodils." Oliver volunteered the information because his mother still looked as if she was steaming.

"They are gorgeous on the walkway," Ashley said appreciatively. "You know there was a poem about them, called the Daffodil Poem? I only remember the lines "I wandered lonely as a cloud, That floats on high o'er vales and hills, When all at once I saw a crowd, A host, of golden daffodils..."

"I know it too. We had to recite it at school. It's by William Wordsworth," Oliver grinned. "I can give you a couple of plants."

"Thank you, Oliver." Ashley smiled at him. "I am very happy that you are not mixed up in this situation."

Honey lost her militant stance when Ashley said that. Her hands, which were curled in defiance, fell to her side.

"Goodbye." Ashley walked toward the gate, stopping to look at the plants before getting into the car.

His mother looked at Oliver when they drove off. "You are sure that you never touched this girl?"

"Yes." Oliver rolled his eyes. "Unless I was asleep or something."

Her lips trembled a tiny bit, a barely perceptible movement, that showed how the news must have affected her.

"Do you think Conroy slept with her?"

"I don't know, Mom."

"But you think it's possible?" Honey whispered.

Oliver sighed. "I don't know. I just don't know."

Chapter Fourteen

Church again. Regina slid into the back row and looked around. The attendance was looking more scanty than usual this morning.

She had left Primrose Hill exactly five weeks ago but she hadn't missed it. She had vowed not to come back but unfortunately she had left her things in the guesthouse, including her house keys. She knew that Lynette would be at church and sitting at the back. It was her usual place.

She was just going to pick up her keys and collect her things, especially her beloved expensive camera that was in her suitcase, and then leave. She had two more weeks of vacation. She would spend it in a place that was not so dangerous to her well-being.

The doctor had told her that she had shown an acute reaction to something up here and that she should be very cautious with everything until she could figure it out. She was not going to take that chance again.

She slid beside Lyn, who gave her a broad, happy smile. It struck Regina that Lyn maybe the only person in Primrose Hill that would give her that welcoming smile.

Ashley obviously had not taken her warnings about Ruel seriously and was still with him. She had gone out on a limb and appealed to Brandon, of all the people in the world, to talk some sense into her but she had not heeded the warning.

She was sorry that she had intervened in Ashley's twisted, messed-up world. She didn't want somebody who would prefer to stay with a murderer than come with her. Even though she loved Ashley to the point of obsession and would do anything for her, this exit strategy for Ashley was something she would have to put on hold for now.

"Hey you," Lyn whispered, "you missed a lot while you were gone."

Regina frowned. "Like what?"

Lyn chuckled. "Jorja, the pastor's daughter, is pregnant."

Regina groaned. "Don't tell me that the father is Oliver. I liked him."

"Oliver? No." Lyn shook her head. "Girl...you'll be surprised when you hear this but my friend Hilma who works at the clinic overheard Honey Allen on the phone asking Conroy Coke if he was the one responsible for the pregnancy. Apparently there are several candidates."

Regina's eyes widened.

"And the first elder's name is on the list." Lyn almost smacked her lips in glee. "Owen Kincaid is in trouble."

"No," Regina whispered, "that can't be true."

"I more than believe it." Lyn's eyes were shining with excitement. "Didn't I tell you that I saw his computer? He loves teenage girls. He has all sorts of naked young girls on there; they look like they are barely of age. Maybe he is acting out his fantasies."

"That's sad," Regina murmured, "if it's true. I don't take delight in hearing these kind of things, Lyn."

"But then again it could be Conroy Coke," Lyn said, ignoring Regina. "He has been celibate for years. Maybe the celibacy got too much for him."

"Lyn!" Regina growled. "I just want my keys. I am going to get the rest of my things and go. There's a yacht party I want to attend tonight. I need to get back in Kingston before they leave the harbor."

Lyn cut her eyes at Regina. "You have become a sour puss. Don't you realize that the mighty Kincaids are about to fall? Didn't you say you were going to out them?"

"I don't care about them anymore," Regina said. "If there is a God, he will surely not allow this lot to be working in his church. He will reveal all some day."

"There is a God," Lyn said sternly. "There is no 'if' about it."

"Okay, okay, there is a God. Gimme the keys."

Lyn fished out the keys out of her bag and handed them to Regina. "You can leave them underneath the front mat when you are leaving."

"Thanks. Bonne chance, Lyn."

"What does bonne chance mean?" Lyn held onto her hand.

"It means good luck."

Lyn smiled. "Bonne chance to you too, Regina. I wish you all the best in the future."

Regina nodded and slipped out of church just when somebody announced that they were going to start praise and worship.

And despite her attempt at being inconspicuous, she was surprised at the door by Norma Kincaid, who was dressed in red from her broad, gaudily decorated hat to her four-inch high red heels, which had some sparkly things on the heels.

Her son was behind her, his beady little eyes watching her, too, with a deadpan expression.

"Morning." Regina's attempt to pass swiftly by was aborted by Norma Kincaid.

"You!" Norma hissed in a condescending tone. "I hope you are not up here to create any more trouble."

Josiah Coke was walking through a side door with some papers in his hand and he paused, looking at the two of them with puzzlement in his eyes.

Regina's blood boiled. She had been prepared to let this evil creature continue to swan about like a generous Christian saint, but the disdain in her voice was almost too much for her.

"You are a hypocrite," Regina hissed, "a sick hypocrite and when I leave here I am going to tell the police all about you."

"How dare you?" Norma Kincaid growled. "How dare you speak to me like that, you filthy..."

"Ma," Jack was hanging on to her arm urgently.

"Oh, so the handicap can speak," Regina laughed, "imagine that. He is the one that is restraining you from blowing your cover. Whatever would the saints say when they see Norma Kincaid acting like a shrew right in the front of the church door?"

Norma's lips were trembling with rage. Her husband came onto the foyer, took in the tableau and walked up to his wife's side.

"What's going on here?"

"I don't know; your wife just attacked me." Regina shrugged. She saw Ruel and Ashley walking toward them from the side door, and she raised her voice a bit. "She is accusing me of stirring up trouble but I am not the hypocrite who watches child porn and may or may not have knocked up the pastor's kid. Maybe she should check with you about the trouble bit."

Owen recoiled in shock and Ruel's steps faltered before he reached the group.

Regina was on a high. She could really believe in this God business because Honey Allen had just parked her car beside Conroy Coke's in the church yard.

Honey nodded to Conroy stiffly and was advancing to the church foyer at a stiff trot, with Oliver behind her.

Conroy was trying to catch up to her and she walked even faster. All the players were in one spot. She put her hands at her side and watched as the group got bigger.

"Regina," Ruel was the first speak, "don't do this here. There is a right way to do things and this is not it."

"Wife killer!" Regina hissed. "Don't speak to me about the right way of doing things. You got rid of that violent nut of a wife as soon as you could, didn't you?"

"Regina!" Ashley gasped.

"Stop acting all shocked," Regina growled at Ashley. "I cared about you enough to warn you about him, but here you are, still with this clown. I got the message, Ashley my ex-lover. Why don't you leave this batch of hypocrites and come back to Kingston with me so that we can finally be together?"

Honey Allen was the first to gasp.

Regina chuckled. "Such deceit and cover-ups huh, Honey. Take you, for instance, you are not even married. You never were. You were living in sin with what's-his-name in Kingston, holding out for a ring.

"The name Allen is fake, to give you some element of respectability. You might not even know who the kid's father is, Conroy or that other guy. Whoever it is, please just give the kid his father's proper name. Every child deserves that."

Honey swung away from the foyer without a word.

"Don't leave, Honey," Regina chuckled, "in the whole scheme of things you are pretty respectable in this group. Norma Kincaid here is much worse than you. She is a human trafficker. She has her little storefront set up to look like she is an employment agency. Then she sets up the unsuspecting people with jobs that are nothing more than modern day slavery.

"I don't know what is worse, Ruel killing his wife or Norma selling poor people to the highest bidders or Owen Kincaid and Conroy Coke sleeping with the pastor's sixteen year old girl. You are all sick, the lot of you."

"Shut up!" Norma screeched. "Shut up now! Shut up this minute! Just shut up!"

That brought the attention of the few people were inside the church.

"You can't shut me up, human trafficker. I will be the specter on your backs, the conscience you can't quench," Regina said. "I will be leaving for now but let it be known that there should be some legal intervention for the lot of you up here and I may be the only one to do it. Ironic isn't it, the sinner getting help for the saints?

Are you coming, Ashley? For once choose me."

"Just leave, Regina." Ashley's voice was trembling. "Just go and don't come back. Ever!"

*****

Silence greeted Regina's departure. And then, one by one, they turned toward their cars. No eye contact was made. The foyer, which was full a minute ago, was now empty except for Oliver, who was feeling stricken, almost as bad as his mother had looked, and Josiah, who was still clutching the papers in his hand.

They looked at each other and neither spoke.

"Good morning gentlemen," Pastor Nolan walked in the foyer with a happy smile on his face.

Oliver opened his mouth to say morning but couldn't.

Josiah recovered faster than he did. "Good morning, Pastor."

"It is scanty today, isn't it?" Nolan asked, still oblivious to the shattering exposé that just took place.

It had been gory enough for there to be some sort of physical evidence to follow in its wake, but there was nothing. Nolan went inside the church and Oliver moved closer to Josiah.

"Do you... er... could it...you think..." He couldn't formulate the rest of the question.

"No," Josiah said. He too was obviously having difficulty processing what just happened. "It can't be true. Obviously."

"Obviously," Oliver said doubtfully. "I should go home and check on my mom."

"Okay." Josiah nodded. "Want me to come with you?"

"No. I, ah...I have this." Oliver walked down the steps and then looked back at the foyer. Josiah was still standing in the same position with a frown on his face.

"You okay?" He felt obligated to ask.

"No," Josiah said, shaking himself back to alertness. "Not at all."

"You think I should go now?" Oliver asked weakly. He was not ready to face his mom yet.

He was afraid to hear Regina's story confirmed and ashamed to admit that if his mother denied it he would not believe her. Her face had looked guilty when Regina had so inelegantly and with flourish revealed her long-held secret.

"You want to?" Josiah took a kerchief out of his pocket and wiped his face.

"Not right now." Oliver walked back up the steps. "I think I will chill out here for a while, soak up some peace."

"Me too." Josiah inhaled raggedly. "Me too."

Chapter Fifteen

"**A**shley, you know she is lying, right?" Ruel walked behind her. Desperation tinged his voice.

"What's going on?" Jorja asked, shocked to see them trotting back inside right after they left for church.

Ruel gave Jorja a look of disdain. "You need to tell us who your baby's father is, Jorja, and stop the games."

Jorja shook her head. "I am not ready to talk about him."

"Fine." Ruel walked toward the room. "I have bigger problems right now."

Jorja walked behind him and saw Ashley dragging clothes from the closet and throwing them into her bag.

"Would somebody mind telling me what's going on?" Jorja asked plaintively.

Ashley looked up from throwing her clothes in the bag. "Ask your father."

Ruel looked at Ashley helplessly. "I did not kill Rosalie. Her former friend Regina is trying to make trouble and apparently I am a murderer. I would never ever do something like that. Ashley, please look at me."

Ashley paused from frantically throwing clothes into a bag.

"Even if I did kill my wife, how would Regina know?"

"She had an investigator looking into all your lives. She has files on you."

Jorja gasped from the doorway. "Really?"

"Leave," Ruel said harshly. "And don't for one minute think that you are off the hook."

"But I don't think you killed Mommy," Jorja said. "Shouldn't that count for something? Unlike your loving wife, I know for sure that you didn't. I believe in you, Daddy."

Ruel looked at his daughter sharply. "You do?"

"Of course, Dad," Jorja said simply. "You wouldn't hurt a fly. I grew up with you and her. I know that Mommy was not the best person to live with and if you didn't kill her when she drew a knife on you in the church parking lot when I was seven or when she almost burned down the house when I was nine or when she..."

"Enough." Ashley sat on the bed and put her hand in her head. "Okay I get it. Ruel was longsuffering."

"And I didn't kill her," Ruel said simply, sitting on the bed beside her. "Regina is seriously poison. Something should be done about her, for her to spew all those lies about everybody."

Jorja frowned. "What did she say?"

Ruel looked at his daughter assessingly. "You tell me your secret and I'll tell you theirs."

Jorja moved away from the door. "I'll be in my room."

"Did you really sleep with Conroy and Owen?" Ruel asked, feeling angry all over again, but this time at his daughter.

Jorja backed away. "I'll leave you two to work out your ...er ...issues."

"Jorja! Get back here!" Ruel stood up and heard the room door slam.

"Can we go back to church?" Ruel asked Ashley. "Staying home is admitting guilt, and I am not guilty of what she is accusing me of."

Ashley sighed. "She outed me in front of those people."

"She said a lot of things about everybody," Ruel said soothingly. "Do you really believe that anybody from that group is now at home saying, 'Sister Ashley had a girl for an ex-lover'?"

"Well, no," Ashley frowned, "but do you really think any of what she said was remotely true?"

Ruel shook his head. "I am not sure, but she did say she would be sending the law up here. That should send the guilty scattering."

*****

When Oliver arrived home in the evening, all the lights were off. His mother's room door was ajar and she was lying on her bed in the same church dress from that morning.

"Mom." He advanced toward her to make sure that she was breathing.

"Oliver." She turned around on the bed slowly, like an old woman with creaky bones.

Oliver sat on the bed beside her. "Pastor Nolan preached today. His topic was Such Were Some Of You. His key text was 1 Corinthians 6: 9-11. You know it?" Oliver asked his mother.

"I don't remember," Honey said faintly.

Oliver chuckled. "Luckily for you, I remember things

verbatim. It says, 'Know ye not that the unrighteous shall not inherit the kingdom of God? Be not deceived: neither fornicators, nor idolaters, nor adulterers, nor effeminate, nor abusers of themselves with mankind, Nor thieves, nor covetous, nor drunkards, nor revilers, nor extortioners, shall inherit the kingdom of God. And such were some of you: but ye are washed, but ye are sanctified, but ye are justified in the name of the Lord Jesus, and by the Spirit of our God.'"

Oliver said gently, "Even the early Christian church had problems and some of those things don't sound so good, do they? Like this morning's list of sins in the church foyer.

"The point pastor made was so appropriate; you can't go to heaven and continue with these behaviors. It was a good sermon."

Oliver lay down at his mother's feet and looked up into the dark ceiling.

"Pastor Ruel and Sister Ashley came back to church. Everybody else came back later in the day."

"Hmmm," Honey murmured.

"Do you think that Pastor Ruel really killed his first wife?"

Honey snorted. Her voice sounded rusty. "It's crazy... maybe."

"And Aunty Norma a human trafficker?" Oliver grunted. "That's unbelievable. And Uncle Owen a porn lover who may or may not have gotten Jorja pregnant and Uncle Conroy..."

Honey stiffened. "She was right about me, Oliver. That's why I didn't come back to church. I am as guilty as charged."

Oliver sighed. "Are you going to tell me what happened now?"

"I met Peter Scarlett when I was doing my internship at the university hospital. He was very handsome and charming. He was also the janitor on the second floor. I was in lust with him. Seriously in lust. I mean I had sex with him on the first date. It wasn't even a proper date. He bought me a patty and a box of juice on my lunch break. I was like an animal in heat."

"Mom!" Oliver squeaked.

"Yup, that was me. Two weeks after meeting him I moved into his poky little house in a very seedy area near the university. Me, a nurse by profession. The thing is, at the time I didn't care if he was a janitor or not. I was so blinded by sexual attraction that I would not listen to reason from anybody about what I was doing.

"A year after moving in with him, I got pregnant. An accident, really—I was on the pill and had a cold and it messed with the effectiveness of the pill.

"Regina was right, I really wanted him to marry me and finally when I got pregnant I expected a ring but no, that didn't happen. I had a difficult pregnancy and Peter was not very supportive. He had other women with me and gradually when the scales fell from my eyes and I was finally sober enough to listen to what others were saying about him, I heard that he had other children. One of them, a boy by the girl who lived in the shack next to ours, that child was born at almost the same time as you.

"So when I had you I got myself an apartment. Invented a name and a story and I've been living a lie ever since."

"Scarlett," Oliver breathed. "My name is Oliver Scarlett."

Honey had tears in her voice. "Oliver, please don't hate me."

"I don't," Oliver said. "I am disappointed that you didn't tell me who he was, but I don't hate you."

"I might move back to Kingston after this." Honey sniffed. "I was thinking about it anyhow. I just can't face the rest of the community, not after this."

"Did you hear about the other people's stories?" Oliver

asked. "Yours is not that spectacular and they all came back to church and nobody looked perturbed. Not even Aunty Norma, who is the so-called human trafficker. I heard her telling Uncle Conroy that Regina was a pathological liar and prone to storytelling."

Honey chuckled weakly. "She wasn't telling lies about me and I am through with pretending and living a lie. I am still leaving. Conroy and I are through. If he slept with that girl... there is no coming back from that.

"And to be in a paternity lottery with Owen Kincaid—I could never ever forgive that. And after hearing what I did, stringing him along for years, pretending I have a doctor husband in Barbados, he is probably thinking that I am the lowest of the low too. I think I should go overseas and work so that I can help pay for your med school. It won't be cheap, even with a scholarship."

"Mom," Oliver groaned, "one thing at a time."

"Yes, that's what I am going to do," Honey whispered. "I have gotten several offers. I stupidly thought that once you were gone off to college I could come clean with Conroy and then we'd see where that leads. But thanks to Regina my lies are all out in the open. It feels good to be finally able to tell the truth."

"Tell me more about my dad," Oliver insisted.

"He is a liar," Honey hissed. "I don't know anything much about him that's true. The girl who had his baby from next door told me that he was from Treasure Beach in St. Elizabeth. She knew him from there."

"What was her name?" Oliver asked, getting excited.

"Sara." Honey sighed. "Sara something or other. She was not very attractive and she swore like a sailor. She had a boy too. Poor thing will probably grow up to be a criminal or something."

"You think my dad still lives there in the ghetto?"

"Maybe, maybe not." Honey sat up in the bed and turned on the sidelight. "He was a sweet talker and extremely good looking. Maybe he has conned some rich girl out of her money by now and is living in the lap of luxury somewhere else."

Oliver shifted on the bed. "I wish I could see a picture of him."

"I destroyed all evidence of him being in my life." Honey looked at Oliver lovingly. "You have his eyes, though."

"And I have a brother too. That's cool."

Honey snorted. "I am sure you have more than one sibling. If I were you I wouldn't get excited about any of them."

"And family." Oliver was not listening to his mother anymore. He was just imagining a line of family members who would welcome him with open arms if they knew about him.

Chapter Sixteen

Screams in the early part of Sunday morning. Bloodcurling screams that could be heard from as far back as Mango Hill, which was a good mile and a half away. Josiah was in the process of running up the hill when he heard them and tried to find where they were coming from.

Ruel was sitting on his veranda, a cup of tea in hand, contemplating his next move. He was going to lose Ashley and his job for sure when he came clean.

He rocked on the chair and thought about how many times he had lied and how many chances he had missed to come clean with the truth but he knew that the moment he did he would lose everything. He was so preoccupied with his thoughts that when Jorja and Ashley rushed out of the house and came on the veranda they looked at him, puzzled.

"Didn't you hear that?" Ashley asked. She was in her track clothes, ready to go running.

"I heard it," Jorja said, and then she mumbled, "Excuse

me," and ran into the house to find the nearest bathroom.

Ruel could hear her retching from the veranda. He was determined that today was the day that Jorja would 'fess up and tell him about the father of her baby.

He looked at Ashley, a small smile on his mouth; she had her hair in two fat plaits and a headband around it.

"What?"

"That," Ashley said when another scream permeated the air.

Ruel jumped up. "I wonder who it could be?"

"It sounds serious," Ashley said fearfully. "Maybe I shouldn't go jogging this morning."

"I'll go put on some clothes and check it out." Ruel went into the house.

Ashley sat down on the steps and waited for him to come back. He came back dressed in a blue track bottom with a white runner thing at the side and in a sleeveless muscle shirt, which showcased his biceps. He didn't do a lick of exercise and he still looked fit.

"Unfair," she said out loud when Ruel opened the gate for her. "Grossly unfair how I have to be working out like crazy to maintain my body."

Ruel chuckled.

"What were you doing up so early anyway?" Ashley asked. "You never get up earlier than I do."

"I couldn't sleep well." Ruel sighed, "Have a lot on my mind. I am going to have to confront Conroy and Owen about this pregnancy thing. It has been on my mind. I almost did it yesterday, too, but I guess I was so shell-shocked by everything else."

"Suppose one of them did it, or both of them slept with her?" Ashley stretched her neck. "What would you do?"

"I am trying not to think about that." Ruel shook his head.

They heard loud sobbing and a wailing "nooo." When they turned the bend in front of the Skinners' house, Lyn was sobbing in the front driveway, her arm over her head. "Nooo…"

Other people were just arriving at the house. One or two of them were trying to get her to talk.

"Maybe Regina robbed the place," Ashley said jokingly to Ruel.

"She's dead!" Lyn inhaled a shuddering breath and started crying again. "Dead!"

Ashley froze, her head echoing the nooo of Lyn's. It couldn't be Regina she was talking about. Regina was too tough and sneaky to die. Too evil, too calculating. She had friends high up in the police force. She should be in Kingston now, calling one of her police friends and telling them tall tales of Primrose Hill and out of courtesy to her father, someone would stir the local police to come look into it.

They would be harassed for a while and then, when the police found no evidence to support Regina's wild accusations, they would apologize and not return. After that Regina would leave her in peace for another five or so years, when she could expect another upset in her life.

Regina was definitely not dead.

Ashley watched as Ruel went over to Lyn Skinner and she got up from the ground, and she watched as she said the words almost in slow motion, "It's Regina."

Ashley drifted closer, torn between a curious sense of relief and grief, each feeling battling for dominance in her heart. Relief was winning. She was fascinated enough to go closer.

"How did she die?" Her voice was even when she asked Lyn.

Lyn wiped her eyes. "I don't really know. She was just out cold on the settee. Her face was swollen."

Ruel took out his cell phone. "We have to call the police. I am figuring this is now a crime scene. We shouldn't go in there."

He moved away from Lyn and called Inspector Campbell. Primrose Hill didn't have a police station but the neighboring town of Chapelton had one. It was a good twenty minutes' drive from Primrose Hill but the police showed up nearly forty minutes later. By that time most of the residents of Primrose Hill were at the scene.

Ashley felt cold. The news set in about ten minutes later and she realized that it really happened. Josiah found her around the same time and squeezed her shoulders.

"Sad, huh?"

Ashley shrugged. "I am not sure."

"I wonder how she died," Josiah mused.

Ashley shook her head. "I guess after the police do their work we'll know more."

"I heard that she ruffled a few people up at your church," an old man said beside them.

Ashley looked over at him. "Really?"

"Yup," the old man nodded, "I don't think it is a matter of what killed her, but who."

*****

Kingsley Hartley got the call on Monday morning from a distraught Lawyer Tharwick.

"Find out who killed my baby. I have a team of police standing by just waiting for your call." The old man's voice was shaking. "Leave no stone unturned, King. No stone. No expense spared. I want a full report and I want a name. There is a police detective up there named Clarke. He was told to work with you. He is waiting at the house for you to come by. I told him not to do anything until you get there."

"Okay sir." King was speaking confidently but inside he felt deflated. He felt like a prophet. He had told Regina to be careful. He had warned her. He knew messing around with people's pasts could be dangerous.

"Her body is at the university hospital. I ordered an autopsy. The results will be in today. Listen for my call."

"Okay sir," King said again, feeling like a broken record. He held the phone long after the lawyer hung up. It shouldn't be hard to pinpoint who killed Regina. He would just have to find out who from the list of names that he had investigated had the most pressing motive to have her killed.

Before that he would have to walk through Regina's stay at Primrose Hill and her last days. It shouldn't take him long to find out what he wanted to know.

His wife stirred beside him and whispered. "What's wrong?"

"Go back to sleep," King murmured.

She sighed softly. "Be like that."

King kissed her hard on the cheek. "I am going to Primrose Hill for three days."

"Okay," she mumbled. "Call me."

"Yep." King got up and headed to the shower. He felt older than his fifty-five years and a great deal sadder than when he had gotten the call from Lawyer Tharwick. He could barely believe it.

The sense of incredulity continued with him when he entered the Primrose Hill community and when he walked into the house, which he had visited just a few short weeks ago, armed with a report on the church board.

"Where was the body?" he asked Clarke, a short young man who couldn't have possibly met the height or weight requirement of the police force. He was short and fat. He had deferred to King from the moment that he walked through the house on mid-Monday. King was OK with the idea of working with him, so long as he didn't interfere much.

"Right here." Clarke pointed at the long sofa. "She was slumped over the settee. There were no bruises on her neck or any evidence of foul play. Her face was swollen but no trauma to indicate a blow. Nothing was taken from her belongings. She had a suitcase left here that the landlady said she was coming to get. The chief said I should show you the pictures."

He handed King the pictures and he pored over them.

"Interesting."

"What?" Clarke tried to see over his shoulders but King was just too tall for that.

"This." King pointed at the glass on the table. "She was drinking something and her face is swollen, her nose and mouth. See?"

"Yes," Clarke nodded, "the medical examiner did remark that her tongue was also swollen. It seemed like she was drinking something milky too."

"Milky?" King sat down in the same chair that he had sat in before and looked at Regina and told her to be careful.

He shook his head. "Why would Regina, who is allergic to milk, be drinking something milky?"

"I have no idea." Clarke shrugged and sat across from him. "Maybe it is one of those imitation milks, like almond milk or something."

King got up swiftly and Clarke scrambled out of the settee to join him.

"I am going to check her room."

"It was basically clean," Clarke said. "The caretaker lady, Lyn, said that she had been in here and cleaned out the place some days prior to Regina returning. She said that all Regina needed to do was collect her bags. There was nothing in the fridge; the place was pristine when we came through here yesterday."

"Hmmmph," King murmured and looked around the clean room. "Not even a wrinkle on the duvet."

He spotted a drawer on the side table with two keys hanging from it. He opened it. It was empty and clean except for a pen that had the Tharwick law firm's logo.

So Regina had used the drawer, probably to store her papers. The papers that he had given her. A shaft of guilt hit him when he thought about that. He could have made himself unavailable when he heard her request. Maybe then she wouldn't have been up here in Primrose Hill. And she wouldn't have died.

"What time was she found?" King turned to Clarke who was leaning on the door jamb and looking bored.

"The housekeeper said she came in at 6:30 on Sunday morning to retrieve the key and check that everything was okay. The medical examiner estimated death at about seven pm. She also suggested that she was strangled except there were no marks on her. Her luggage was near the door so she had intended to leave."

"Where is it?" King headed to the hall area again.

"Right there." Clarke pointed to it in the corner. "It is locked. We left it for the family… er, you to claim."

King nodded and pulled out the stylish black suitcase from the corner it was in. The lock was an ordinary light padlock.

He opened it in ten seconds using his master key.

"Cool." Detective Clarke looked at the key.

"Interested in a life of crime, Detective?" King grunted as he opened the suitcase.

"No," Clarke said sheepishly.

King looked through Regina's clothing and toiletries and

then he found the report he had done for her at the very bottom of the bag. It was in a black zipped-up folder.

He opened the folder. "Who last saw her alive?"

"Apparently, she went to church the day before and she made a scene," Clarke said, "accusing people of a couple of whoppers. That is currently the hot topic in the district."

"Mmmm," King said, pulling out the files. He scanned through them. Only the files on Ruel Dennison and Honey Allen were in there. Everybody else's was missing. He frowned at that. He was suspicious about that. Why would these two be the only ones remaining?"

He found a piece of paper with her unmistakable scribbling. She had made a list.

He scanned through the list: Norma Kincaid, Owen Kincaid, Ruel Dennison, Honey Allen, Conroy Coke, Josiah Coke, Nolan Ramsey. The seven saints, she had scribbled under that and then all over, she had written ha ha ha ha ha ha ha.

Seven ha's.

His seven suspects, King thought, looking over the names again. One of them had done something to Regina; he was only waiting for the autopsy to find out how.

"What do we do now?" Clarke asked. He was getting restless. As far as he was concerned this was an open and shut case.

"Wait on the autopsy results." King sighed. "I am almost certain that somebody knew of her medical history. Somebody was biding their time. Somebody gave her something to drink and watched as she suffocated and died. That somebody is going to prison if it's the last thing I do."

Chapter Seventeen

It was the most somber board meeting that Ruel could recall chairing. He had called them to an emergency Monday evening session after yesterday's tragic event. He looked from one face to another, and most of them tried to avoid his gaze. Only Nolan Ramsay and Josiah Coke were looking at him with confidence. Honey Allen had barely glanced up from the floor since she walked into the room.

"Let me just say," Ruel's voice was as strident as he could make it, "I did not kill my first wife. Let's get that out of the way. I may be guilty of some things but not murder. We need to address what happened on the doorsteps at our own church the other morning. The accusations. The innuendos. We cannot serve this church with all of these rumors hanging over our heads. We need to clear the air and be truthful with each other, at least."

He sighed. He needed to take this advice himself. He cleared his throat.

"Resign if you have to, but we cannot bring this church into disrepute."

After his speech there was silence.

And then Honey Allen spoke. "She was right about me. I am not hiding that. I am guilty as charged, so I might as well resign."

After she spoke Conroy glanced at her, his gaze veiled. "That's really big of you to admit something like that, Honey. It's a pity you couldn't tell me this years ago. I wanted to marry you."

"And I didn't want my son to think badly of me," Honey said simply. "So I stuck to my story. But surely my situation is not worse than yours. You slept with the pastor's kid. Now how is that for the pot calling the kettle black?"

"I did not!" Conroy said, his eyes flashing. "I am not attracted to her and as much as Jorja looks like an adult, she is still a child. I am shocked and downright dismayed and mystified that this Regina person could come up with these things about me."

Ruel cleared his throat. "Actually, Jorja was the one who mentioned your name first."

Conroy looked puzzled. "I can't imagine why she would say that. I have only ever been nice and supportive to that girl."

"Maybe because you accommodated her little touchy-feely moments," Honey said. "I saw you and her. She was all but draped over you and purring in your ears."

"I don't know what you are talking about," Conroy said, flushed. "I don't know what it is that you think you saw but I was not thinking in that manner. Not about her." Conroy looked at Ruel. "Listen Pastor, I have never had sex with your daughter. Never. I think having to defend myself like this is a very cruel and unusual punishment."

Ruel nodded. He believed him.

Conroy looked as if he was fit to chew nails. "That Regina girl was trying to destroy my reputation and she couldn't have chosen a worse venue."

"Okay Dad, we get it," Josiah said softly. He looked around at the others. "He has been like this since it happened. Regina shocked him with her, er, revelations."

Conroy was still agitated too. "The nerve of that woman."

"She is dead, though," Norma said softly, "so that is something."

Ruel looked at Norma and then Owen.

"I don't have to defend myself," Owen said, blustering when he felt their eyes on him. "This is crazy. I don't have porn on my computer. One time I was looking at some pageant pictures of a girl who wanted our agency to sponsor her. Norma and I decided not to. Those must be the naked pictures Regina was talking about, and I am pretty sure she got that info from Lyn Skinner. I caught her on my computer more than once, looking for what only God knows.

"As for Jorja, I don't know what to say. Like Conroy, I am pretty taken aback by the accusations. I didn't have sex with her; I've only been nice to her. I don't understand!"

Ruel sighed. "So you are totally innocent of the charges levied at you."

Owen eyed him sharply. "Yes, I am!"

"So when you carried Jorja to music class, did you see anything untoward between her and the music teacher, Greg?"

"No." Owen shook his head. "Greg is paralyzed from the waist down; what is there to observe?"

Ruel started drumming his fingers on the table. "Then this is quite the dilemma we are in. My daughter says you both are candidates for her child's paternity."

"I can submit to a DNA test," Owen said without pause. "I am not hiding a thing."

"Me too," Conroy said, "but to imagine that I am going to have to be defending myself for the next couple of months really puts a bad taste in my mouth."

"And mine too," Owen said quickly. "But what can we do?"

Norma had been silent until now. "I just want to say that this is really your fault, Ruel. You should be a proper father to that girl. She is obviously a troublemaker and an awful liar, just like that girl Regina. She needs to be careful. Troublemakers tend to end up dead."

Silence greeted that statement.

"What are you trying to say, Norma?" Ruel asked tensely.

"I said it," Norma hissed. "Rein in your wild child!"

"So are you really a human trafficker Sister Norma?" Nolan asked, looking at Norma innocently.

"I won't even dignify that with a response," Norma said scornfully. "I told Owen already and I am going to tell you all publicly. I find this whole situation to be beneath me. After all the things I have done in this church…for this whole community, you would all listen to the likes of that girl Regina…then all I have to say is y'all are a bunch of ungrateful leeches."

"Sister Norma," Ruel said softly, "we are all just talking here, no need for insults."

"Oh, there is need," Norma said with heat. "I have done many things for this community, this church, each of you here. You all eat at my house; you call me a friend and now this…unbelievable!

"If your wife didn't have a connection to Regina, she wouldn't have been up here poking around in our business and if your promiscuous child did not see it fit to mention my husband on her list of candidates, then my family would not be involved in this madness.

"As I see it, Ruel, the problem begins with you. You! You should resign. Your presence in our community, our church has caused quite the upheaval, wouldn't you say?

"Anyway, if you don't have the balls to resign I will."

She stood up bristling. "I resign from all posts effective immediately. I don't care what you lot want to think, only God is my judge."

She stormed out of the meeting, her head held a notch higher than usual.

Silence greeted her exit.

Owen cleared his throat. "Well, I guess I should go too. I, er, resign effective immediately."

He got up and left quietly.

"That leaves me," Conroy said, "the other person in this, er, paternity question."

He looked at each person seated at the table. "For the next couple of months, I won't be able to hold my head up in this community."

He looked at Honey regretfully. "Life, huh?"

Honey shrugged and picked up her bag. "Life." She paused before she walked out. "Pastor Ruel and Nolan, I wish you all the best in the ministry and I apologize for my lies and any repercussions that my actions may cause this board."

Ruel nodded. "That is brave of you, Honey."

She placed her hand on his shoulders in a gesture of affection. "When you are outed as a wrongdoer sometimes it is a blessing. I think the best thing to do is to acknowledge your faults to others and your sins to God and ask for his forgiveness. It is the best thing to do."

She left and the closing door was the only sound in the room.

Ruel looked at both Josiah and Nolan and then sighed. "I have never overseen such a mass exodus from a church leadership."

"Me neither." Nolan murmured. "But then again I am new to this."

Ruel closed his eyes and when he opened them they were red and wet. "You know, Honey is right. I am going to have to do the same."

"What are you talking about?" Josiah asked urgently. "You didn't do anything wrong."

"Oh yes, I did." Ruel rubbed his hand across his face, his shoulders slumped in defeat. "No, I didn't kill my wife but I did something that was not right. I have to tell Ashley first and then the conference. It is a strong possibility I may no longer be working here at Primrose Hill."

Nolan and Josiah looked at each other.

"Ruel," Josiah said hesitantly.

Ruel stood up. "For the time being, Nolan, you are in charge. Your first order of business is to find yourself a church board."

*****

"Going somewhere, Norma?" King was leaning on her car when he saw Norma storming towards him in the church parking lot.

"Yes." Norma snapped. "What is it, Kingsley Hartley?"

"Regina Tharwick." King straightened himself from the car lazily. His hard, weather-worn features looked deceptively calm.

"What about her?" Norma disarmed the car and reached for the door handle.

King grabbed her arm. "What did you do, Norma? You

were not content with selling people to the highest bidders; now you are into murder?"

"Get your hands off me," Norma said haughtily. "What on earth did you tell that girl about me? I don't sell people and I did not kill Regina Tharwick."

"Her autopsy said that she died from anaphylaxis. An extreme form of allergic reaction. In her case it was peanuts and milk. Well, peanut milk...she almost died from this before. Somebody knew that."

Norma pulled her hand from his roughly. "Sorry for your loss. Now move."

King hissed his teeth. "I gave her a report on seven persons. Only two were still in her belongings, Ruel Dennison and Honey Allen. Now, as I am hearing, your church board has seven persons, so that leaves four files which were taken from her: Norma Kincaid, Owen Kincaid, Conroy Coke and Josiah Coke. The new pastor Nolan Ramsey didn't have a file and is clean."

Norma snorted, "so what?"

"One of you from the four gave Regina peanut milk to drink and then watched her as she suffocated and died. That is heartless...can you imagine that person watched as her throat swelled up, her breathing got labored and she passed out from lack of oxygen? All without touching her. Then someone took the rest of the files. You are my first suspect. It seems like somebody who doesn't want the police snooping into their business would do."

Norma stiffened. "You are barking up the wrong tree, Kingsley Hartley. I own an employment agency, that's all. I am a mere recruiter. I put the right employees with the right employer. Most of them are grateful for my services. Human trafficking is a wild leap from that."

King looked at her coldly. "And you call your self a

Christian. I don't get it."

"And you call yourself a detective," Norma rejoined, "I don't get it."

She levied that barb at King and he stepped back as she got in her car. She rolled down her window.

"You know, the other day when Regina was confidently rattling off her list of wrongdoers, I heard more than four names. There was also Ashley Dennison, her ex-lover.

"And if I were any sort of detective I would find out about Lyn Skinner, her housekeeper and the one with access to the house. Surely you have other people to look into or you are going to let them slide because you are so fixated on me?"

She sneered at King. "You leave my family alone. That is a warning."

*****

Ashley was washing dishes very slowly and staring outside at the landscape. She glanced at the clock. It was a little after six and the sunlight was dancing on the wet leaves outside. The brief shower of rain earlier was welcomed. It was raining every other day now and she was feeling grateful but listless. She couldn't stop thinking about Regina.

It had only just sunk in that she had really disappeared from the face of the earth as she had carelessly said before. Her eyes had become fixated on one particular leaf hanging by just the tiniest string of a spider web.

She watched it as if she was in a trance and was jerked out of her reverie when she heard a knock on her gate. She had to get it, because Jorja had holed herself up in her room all day. She had only stirred to get some food after Ruel left for his emergency board meeting and then had scurried back to her place of solace as if somebody had stones waiting for her at every turn.

She dried her hands on the towel. The tension in the house was so thick it could be cut with a knife.

Yesterday, Jorja hadn't eaten because Ruel was determined that she should talk to him about her pregnancy. Ashley had taken her temperamental car to the garage to avoid the tension in the house.

Ashley felt as if she was watching the drama from afar. She was feeling detached. Detached by Regina's death, detached by Jorja's pregnancy. She was just going through the motions, feeling emotionally drained.

She pulled the curtains and saw a tall, gray-haired gentleman at the gate. He was dressed in a white dress shirt and dark brown pants. He was patiently knocking the gate with little energy. She opened the door and saw that his face had several deep lines on it, especially in the middle of his forehead. He looked like a man that frowned a lot. He also looked tough and he had a military walk. Very erect and purposeful.

"The name is King, Ma'am," he said when she gave him a tentative good evening.

"How may I help you?" Ashley asked, looking down at herself. She was in a ratty cloth track suit that had once been black but was now washed out. Her hair was a mass of frizziness. She didn't have the energy to comb it.

King advanced up the walkway and looked at one of her veranda chairs. "May I sit?"

"Okay," Ashley said ungraciously. Just who was this King?

"I am investigating Regina's death," he answered her silent question. He ran his hand over his face.

Ashley sat on the chair opposite him and looked at him curiously. "How did she die? That has been the question on everybody's lips."

"She had an anaphylactic reaction to peanut milk." King watched her closely when he said it. "Something that could have easily been handled with a shot of epinephrine. Somebody must have given her the milk and watched her as she had a reaction to it."

Ashley kept her face neutral. "Wow."

"The coroner is estimating death at around seven o'clock Saturday evening."

"Ah." Ashley nodded.

"Where were you?" King asked. He had not moved his bloodshot eyes from her. Not even a second. Ashley felt as if she was in a fish bowl.

"Seven o'clock?" Ashley crossed her arms. "I was here, at home. It was after church. Jorja was here too. I guess she can vouch for me."

"Mmm," King murmured. "Where was your husband?"

"He was still at church." Ashley shrugged. "There was a meeting, I think, with some persons who were very disturbed by what Regina had said that morning at church."

"What exactly did she say?" King leaned closer.

Ashley squinted, trying to remember the scene on the church porch. "When I came on the scene, Norma Kincaid was there with her son Jack. Norma was looking really angry. Angrier than I had ever seen her. Oliver Allen was standing with his mouth hanging open and Josiah had a stack of papers in his hand.

"Regina was standing in the middle, flailing her hands. She announced that Ruel was a murderer, Honey Allen was a liar, Conroy Coke and Owen Kincaid were guilty of sleeping with Jorja—that's Ruel's kid—and that I was her ex-lover."

"Mmm." King flexed his fingers. "How did that make you feel?"

Ashley shrugged. "I just wanted her to shut up, as Norma

was yelling for her to do."

"Did you want her dead?" King was not beating around the bush, obviously.

"No." Ashley looked him in the eye. "Not then. I can't speak for the past, though. Sometimes, I would practically wish it and now that she is gone, I feel so...numb. She was poison for me, a stalker. She wouldn't leave me alone but... death is so final and so...I don't know...I am not sure what to feel."

"Mmmm." King leaned back in his chair.

"If only she had just left quietly instead of so dramatically in typical Regina style, she would still be alive now. I wouldn't feel so..."

"Guilty." King finished hoarsely.

"Maybe there is a bit of guilt," Ashley said. "She'd be alive if she hadn't followed me up here. Do you really think somebody fed her peanut milk?"

"Yes." King nodded. "Somebody who knows of her allergies."

"That would be everybody." Ashley looked at King, "Regina had a reaction to something or the other and they carried her to the clinic. Honey Allen has been telling everyone who cared to listen that Regina was ill and what may have caused it."

King sighed. "Thank you, Honey Allen, for giving someone the perfect murder weapon."

Chapter Eighteen

Day two. King was not finding it easy to prove his theory that Regina was murdered and that did not sit well with his police friends and the head detective Barnes in particular.

His theory was touted as too far-fetched and ridiculous. The head detective had told him as much.

"Who would want to kill her, really, Mr. Hartley? She was just a visitor to the area. Primrose Hill residents are the quietest, most law-abiding citizens in Jamaica. No one would ever think to do such a thing. What happened was tragic and not usually seen but obviously it was an accident. She drank peanut milk and died."

He was leaning back in his chair, an indulgent smile on his face as he regarded King, and that set his teeth on edge. Barnes was a toddler compared to him and yet he was treating King as if he was some dimwitted child.

"They have motive," King grunted. "The pastor is a murderer. He killed his first wife."

"Allegedly. Based on deductions that you fed to Miss Tharwick that have no basis in reality."

King didn't want to hear that. He realized that he had made some broad suppositions and had given them to Regina, but he was almost sure he was right about Ruel.

"The first elder slept with the pastor's daughter."

"Allegedly," Barnes pointed out with vigor. "Owen Kincaid is a man of impeachable stature in the community. That is a really wild accusation that Miss Tharwick announced to the public."

"But was it wild enough to get her killed?" King asked.

Barnes narrowed his eyes. "But why kill her? The information was already out in the open and is easily provable or disprovable in nine months?"

"Maybe he didn't want anybody poking around their business." King was getting frustrated and it was showing in his voice. "They own an employment agency that is facilitating modern day slavery."

"Do you have proof?" Barnes folded his arms and looked at King lazily.

"Of course," King nodded, "I have a few persons who have been placed by Norma Kincaid who can tell you what she does. She carries her victims to Kingston. They have an agent there; his name is Briggs. He does a physical of the candidate. They are treated well. They then travel with Norma Kincaid to the States, where another agent takes over. He assigns them jobs all over the world. They work and are bound to him for years. They have to pay almost sixty percent of their checks over to this agent.

"After a few years they are offered some options, give a kidney, work at a strip club—that sort of thing—and then you'll be free. If that isn't human trafficking I don't know what is."

"Hmm." Detective Barnes nodded. "If you can bring in some witnesses I will have somebody verify the allegations."

"Good," King murmured. "Josiah Coke is next on the list."

"What did Josiah do?" Barnes refrained from rolling his eyes but King could see that he was close to doing so. Barnes was making it obvious that he was humoring him.

"He got his job through Norma Kincaid."

"Is he one of your witnesses for this human trafficking?" Barnes was enjoying himself now, and King was reminded briefly why he disliked dealing with the country police. They were all a bunch of sycophants and amateurs.

"No." King frowned. "Josiah Coke is a financial prodigy. He was working for Prism Financials and then he stopped suddenly and returned here to live. He single-handedly built up his father's fledgling farm. I am still ascertaining why he left but I believe it had something to do with money laundering."

"Tell you what." Barnes had the gall to wink at him. "When you have solid evidence against these people and not vague beliefs and innuendos, I will be prepared to do something about it. In the meantime, the chief okayed you to have Clarke for two more days as a courtesy to lawyer Tharwick. If you find nothing by tomorrow you are on your own."

He got up, signifying the conversation to be over, and led King through the dingy hallways of the station and out into a bleak grey day.

"It's gonna rain." Clarke joined him outside the station. He was eating a sandwich. "We need it, all we can get."

"We also need a solid lead in this case," King murmured.

"Say, did you check where the brand of peanut milk that she was drinking was sold?"

"It's a popular brand." King shrugged. "Everybody sells it. The housekeeper has a case of it in her top cupboard."

"Mmm." Clarke walked behind him. "Well, there is an easy way to get this cleared up, if you are sure that it's murder as you said."

"What way?" King asked. He was feeling surly.

"You won't like it." Clarke warned. "It is not in any police procedural book ever written."

"Just get to the point," King snapped at him.

"You can cast lots," Clarke said cautiously. "I have seen it done; it works. You have so many suspects and they all go to the same church. Maybe you can have God solve the mystery for you."

King stopped and looked at Clarke, searching to see if he had lost his mind.

"No, I will not cast lots. I am a detective. I detect and I am going to solve this case by tomorrow."

"From your mouth to God's ears," Clarke murmured.

*****

King's first stop for the day was Honey Allen. She was not at home but her son was. He was repotting some of the yellow flowers at the front. He said his name was Oliver and he politely offered him something to drink.

King declined. The boy was not a suspect, and though he didn't have any known allergies he was not going to eat or drink anything from the people of Primrose Hill.

"Where was your mother at seven Saturday evening?" King cut to the chase quickly.

"In bed," Oliver said easily. "She left church earlier that morning, and when I got in she was in bed. She hadn't moved since Regina lambasted her in front of everyone."

Oliver shrugged. "That was mean of Regina. I liked her but that scene was ugly."

King nodded impatiently. "What time did you get home from church?"

"Six-ish." Oliver frowned. "Why?"

"Did you pass by the Skinners' house?" King asked, willing the boy to say yes.

"Yes." Oliver nodded. "I did."

King did a jig in his head. *Yes!*

"Did you see anything unusual about the house?"

"No," Oliver said and then frowned. "Well, not the house exactly."

"Then what?" King couldn't hide the eagerness from his voice.

"I thought it odd when I saw Jack at the top of the hill. He walked with me to the gate here and then went back." Oliver shook his head. "It had just struck me as off at the time. Maybe because Jack is usually at church with his parents, but I guess it wasn't that odd since they didn't return for the evening program. So neither did he."

"That's Jack Kincaid?" King confirmed.

"Yes." Oliver nodded, "apart from that though, it was an ordinary evening."

"Thank you." King nodded to Oliver. "You have been a big help."

"You are welcome, I guess." Oliver went back to his plants and King moved away, his heart singing; he had a lead and he was almost certain now what had happened. He looked at his watch; he had agreed to meet Clarke at the Skinners' house in fifteen minutes.

Lyn Skinner had agreed to meet them there.

Chapter Nineteen

Ruel was dressed and on the veranda in the early part of the morning. He hadn't slept a wink that night. He knew what he had to do. He had known from the very day that he saw Ashley and lusted after her that he couldn't have her but he had thrown all caution to the wind and now...it was time to let her go or beg her stay.

He shuddered and the morning wasn't even cold. Every day he had thought about it and every day he said one more day.

One more day.

One more day.

Until he was one year into his relationship with her. A year he wouldn't forget. He still thought that she was perfect for him but it had come too late, for both of them. She was not going to be happy with him when he told her. She was going to feel deceived. Today she was going to feel lied to and betrayed. He couldn't spare her that.

Today was the day when he would lose everything important to him. Maybe, just maybe, he could delay the inevitable for one more day, but he squashed that thought. It wouldn't be fair that Nolan, the young pastor, would be left to sink in his second month on the job.

It wouldn't be fair to his congregation; some of them were already shaken by the accusation that he killed his first wife.

It wouldn't be fair to Jorja, who obviously needed guidance. He couldn't offer her the guidance and support she needed when he was so caught up in his own situation. He had already failed in his relationship with her.

He would confess to both Jorja and Ashley and then he would call the conference. He got up and stretched and inhaled the faint tinge of orange blossom in the air.

He then went inside and headed to Jorja's room door. He knocked softly but didn't get a response. He turned the doorknob and was surprised to see that it wasn't locked. She had done her fair share of locking him out these past couple of days.

He walked toward her bed. She was snoring lightly, her mouth half opened. The sheets were tangled and hanging half off the bed.

The fan made a rattling groan in the corner of the room. His little girl. Ruel felt a surge of regret; he had not shaped up to be the best father in the world, had he?

He sat beside her bed and pulled one of her braids from her face.

She stirred and snuffled but didn't wake up. He saw a book marked 'diary' on her side table. And his hand itched to pick it up.

And he did. Her penmanship was atrocious. The book opened up on August 12th, yesterday. Ruel read the entry in the book and then put it back down, his heart pounding in weird staccato beats.

He inhaled shakily and then exhaled in a huge plunge of air.

Jorja woke up. "Dad?" She blinked at him blearily.

"Yes, it's me." Ruel sighed. "I wanted to talk."

"Not about my pregnancy," Jorja groaned and turned her head away.

"No." Ruel sighed. "I want to talk about your mother... and then, about your pregnancy."

Jorja turned over and looked at him. "Okay."

*****

King had to admit that when he met up with Clarke he was no longer interested in Lyn Skinner. He waited at the entrance to the Skinner home impatiently. He was more interested in Jack Kincaid right now, Norma Kincaid's little handyman. She must have sent him to kill Regina. His instructions would be simple. Feed Regina the peanut milk and don't leave until she stops breathing.

That woman had a lot to answer for. His resentment boiled over. He didn't want to acknowledge that he had a personal vendetta against Norma Kincaid. He couldn't tell anybody that. He hadn't wanted to let Regina know that he had only taken her case when he heard where she was staying and that Norma Kincaid was involved.

He had a personal desire to see Norma Kincaid fall flat on her face.

Back when he was a young man of twenty-five and couldn't read or decipher a word of English, he had gone to an adult learning class at the local church school in May Pen. His teacher was Norma Landis, a twenty-year-old girl who had volunteered to teach them for two weeks.

He had attended because it was free. Norma had done it because she was broke but she could read really fluently. She had no teacher training, nor tact or diplomacy. She had looked him in the eye one night after he struggled with his vowels and told him that he wouldn't amount to anything. She had sneered at him and called him dunce.

He had never forgotten it. Her words had hurt but that sneer had dwelt with him for thirty years and ever since then he had been interested to see when she was going to fall.

Today was the day. He almost rubbed his hands in glee.

"What are you looking so pleased about?" Clarke asked curiously.

"I have a lead." King could barely contain his pleasure.

"Oh." Clarke nodded. "No need to cast lots then?"

"No need."

"You are good." Clarke whistled. "It usually takes us weeks to find a reliable lead."

King grunted. He swallowed the insult he had for the police force. He had once been a member and he had had a fruitless twenty years.

Since he prematurely retired and started his own investigation business, he was just beginning to see results. He preferred this to the endless bureaucracy and unsolved cases.

He still needed the law though, because he could see in his mind's eye Clarke slapping the handcuffs on Norma Kincaid and her whole family.

Lyn Skinner walked up the road and spotted them. They met her at the gate.

"How are you, Miss Skinner?" Clarke asked amiably.

"Fine and a bit sad. I didn't know her that well but what I knew I liked. Regina was a tough bird," Lyn whispered. Her voice was hoarse and low. "I broke my voice screaming out on Sunday. I didn't expect to see her in the house, you know. She said she had a yacht party that she needed to go to from Saturday night and then to see that she was dead…"

King nodded. "The place was not broken into so whoever Regina let into the house was someone she knew."

"Or the door was opened," Lyn said. "She was leaving; she just said that she was going to get her bag. Maybe if I had just come to check that she was really gone then she could have gotten help before she passed out. The last time she had an allergy it took her nearly an hour to be swollen and rashy. What I can't understand is why would she drink something that she is allergic to?"

"Maybe somebody wanted her gone." King pushed his hand in his pocket and rocked back on his heels.

Lyn Skinner nodded. "She really went ham on them at church. She told me before that she had had it and she would have nothing more to do with Primrose Hill. I was even telling her some rumors about the pastor's girl but she said she didn't want to hear it. Next thing I know she met Norma Kincaid on the step and all hell broke loose."

"You heard the whole thing?" King asked.

"Well, close enough," Lyn said. "I was sitting on the very back of the church bench to the right near the door, and Regina was not subtle at all."

"You were the Kincaid's housekeeper for years. How would you say they are?"

Lyn sighed. "They are good people. I was jealous and wrong and frustrated with my lot in life and I stole from them. If I hadn't met Regina and poured out my bitterness to her, she wouldn't have wanted to stay. This is a wake-up call detectives. I have stopped gossiping and pointing fingers. Regina's death was a sign for me to stop."

"Ridiculous," King snorted when Lyn Skinner turned

toward the house.

"Death and life are in the power of the tongue," Clarke said softly. "She's right. She may have started a chain of events that did not have to happen."

"But calling the Kincaids good just because she has come to some awareness is ridiculous." King sputtered. "By the way, that's where we are going next. A witness said their boy, Jack Kincaid, was loitering around here the evening of her death."

Chapter Twenty

Ruel left Jorja in her room sobbing and he rubbed his trembling arms across his face. Next stop Ashley.

After that the Cokes' hydroponics farm.

After that he didn't know what else. Maybe a long fasting and prayer session where he would, like David, his favorite character in the Bible, ask the Lord to cleanse him with hyssop and make him clean again. He knew one thing for certain; he would probably not go back into the ministry in a formal position. He would probably teach; after all, he had a degree in education.

Ashley was asleep when he pushed the door and went into the room. It was quite unusual for her to be asleep at this hour, but he didn't move any farther into the room to wake her up. There was time enough for that. He went back to the living room, grabbed his Bible and tightly closed his eyes. *Lord, give me strength, please.*

"Oh my, look at the time!" Ashley came out to the living

room a half hour later, looking frazzled. "Why didn't you wake me up, Ruel? It's nine o'clock!"

Ruel looked at her, a misty smile on his face. "You needed the rest."

Ashley was in one of those slip-looking nightdresses that rode up on her legs when she lifted her hands.

He drank her in; he might never see her like this again.

"I need to talk to you."

She looked at him and blinked. "I am not seeing straight and I need to brush my teeth. Give me five minutes."

"Sure." Ruel smiled calmly at her but inside he was quaking. The threat of imminent loss overtook him and when she came back and sat across from him, folding her legs beneath her, and looked at him with her beautiful limpid eyes, the words had fled.

"I didn't kill Rosalie."

Ashley smiled gently. "Ruel, you've said it so many times. I believe you. I know Regina had her theories."

"I didn't kill her because she is not dead."

He waited for that news to sink in.

"Explain." Ashley's lips trembled. "I don't get it."

Ruel grimaced. "We were supposed to go to Florida on vacation. Well, not really vacation. I wanted a second opinion about her mental condition because she was not getting better and I heard about this doctor there who was good with people like Rosalie. Before we could board the plane Rosalie attacked one of the security officials. The metal detector went off and she was patted down and that triggered one of her rages. They couldn't calm her down. It was chaos. Instead of jail she was taken to the mental hospital at Bellevue."

"Oh God." Ashley sank down to the bed. "What?"

"She had to be forcibly sedated," Ruel whispered, "and then they admitted her after a battery of tests. She was deemed to be a threat to herself and others and was admitted. That was where I spent my so-called vacation," Ruel said ruefully. "It was while there that I came up with this obviously ill-thought-out idea to announce her death. You see, I reasoned that if I said she was dead then I would be free to explore the overwhelming feelings I had toward you. I knew you were going to be at the convention so I made sure that I showed up there. I knew you were divorced. I knew you had children and that they didn't live with you and that you weren't seeing anybody. I basically stalked you for months before that and when Rosalie finally snapped, I hatched a foolproof plan for us to be together."

"Dear God." Ashley squeezed her eyes shut. "How could you be as devious as to try to cover up something like this? Did you think that this could be swept under the carpet forever? I am not really married to you, am I?"

"No," Ruel whispered, "I am afraid not."

"I can't process this." Ashley closed her eyes and then she started chuckling. And then the chuckle turned into a full-blown laugh that she couldn't quite stop.

"Ashley," Ruel said softly, "please forgive me, I..."

"No," Ashley growled, straightening up and wiping her eyes. "No sentiments please. I fully and totally understand that this is my punishment. Justice is served. I had a perfectly good husband, I cheated on him, I deceived him and I continually lied to him. I hurt him in horrible ways and now only now I understand what I did to Brandon. This is my just reward."

"I started divorce proceedings a year ago with Rosalie. It was finalized six weeks ago, when Regina came by."

"You started divorce proceedings when we had our bogus wedding? So many people deceived." Ashley sighed tiredly. "I would just like to go back to sleep and forget that this year happened."

"Ashley..." Ruel wanted to plead with her to forgive him, to stay with him, to sort this madness out, to marry him for real this time, but Ashley was not really listening.

She half-opened her eyes. "I am going to have to pack. My car is at the mechanic. How am I going to get out of here? Better yet, how am I going to forget that this happened? I am not really married. I have Dennison on all my legal documents. So many things to sort out, so many people to explain to."

"Ash, please. We could get married for real tomorrow. I want you to know that I still love you...I really do love you..."

"No thanks," Ashley said softly, in that half asleep quality that she had adopted. "I am going to summon the energy to pack and then I am going to leave here today. Have you told Jorja that her mother is still alive?"

"Yes." Ruel nodded. "She took it pretty well."

"I can't imagine how she could take that news well." Ashley got up and grimaced. "It's her mother..."

"Her mother was not healthy and was a danger to us all. Jorja understands that."

"There is no justification, Ruel...you think you know a person...you can't just take people at face value anymore, can you?"

Ruel sighed. "We all have our secret dark things, even you..."

"I thought you were different...perfect."

"I am a man and fallible," Ruel said. "I can only be perfect through Jesus Christ and without him I am completely and spectacularly fallible, but I am coming clean and I need to know how you feel about us."

Ashley shook her head. "I can't... this is too much."

"I am going to the Cokes' farm now," Ruel said gently, "do

you want a lift to Kingston when I get back?"

"No, I am sure I can manage." Ashley didn't even look at him as she headed for the room again. It was over. No fanfare. No dramatics. No feeling. And that, more than anything, was heartbreaking.

*****

King and Clarke drove up at the Kincaids' house at the same time Norma was backing out her vehicle. She stopped when King alighted from the car and got out of the vehicle, looking angry.

"You don't give up, do you?" She looked at King angrily. "What is it now?"

"Mrs. Kincaid," King said, satisfaction lacing his voice, "I am here to see your son."

Norma frowned, "Jack? Why?"

"He was seen near the Skinner house at the time of Regina's unfortunate demise."

Norma frowned fiercely. "So what?"

King had her. She looked cornered and slightly afraid, though she was hiding it well. Her little plot was foiled.

"May we see him, ma'am?" Clarke asked gently. "We just have some questions for him."

King was not into the gentle courteousness. He wanted to see Norma Kincaid knocked down a notch or two. He wanted to see her bleed. He almost growled in her face, "Get him now."

Norma jumped but she meekly complied, hurrying toward the sprawling house as if dogs were at her heels.

When she returned with the boy, Owen Kincaid was also with him.

Owen greeted them cordially, King noted. He was quite

the gentleman. King had to give him that. He was not as blustery and waspish as his wife.

"Jack Kincaid," King said, observing the boy in slight disbelief. He was thin and tall and looked as if a good gust of wind could blow him away. He was also bashful. He tried to unsuccessfully hide behind his mother but he was taller than she was and his actions looked comical.

"How old are you?" King didn't even realize that he was asking it out loud. In his imagination he pictured a young, stropping adult who was able to force Regina to drink something she was allergic to and intimidate her into staying until she suffocated to death.

"Ma," the adult kid whined to his mother.

"Answer." Norma looked at her son sternly.

The boy hung his head and murmured, "Twenty-one."

King's previous conclusions were looking very dim now. Was this man/child capable of harming anyone?

"Why were you at the Skinner's place?" King growled and watched him flinch.

"There is no need to speak to him like this," Norma rounded on King, defending her son. "He does not respond well to bullying and that is what you are doing, Mr. Hartley."

King had to give a mental nod. He was being harsh but part of that was frustration. He had so wanted this kid to be the one to be culpable for the crime.

"I followed Josiah," the kid said hesitantly. "His car was at the Skinners' house in the morning. I... I saw him when we were heading back to church after that girl made Ma cry."

"He doesn't need to know that," Norma said, holding her chin high. "Just stick to what you saw."

"And in the evening, I saw him walking by. He never walks by on church day. So I followed him and I saw when he went over to the Skinners' place. He went over to the side window and looked through."

King's eyes connected with Norma's and he realized that they were both thinking the same thing.

"And then he came out of the yard. He didn't see me because he headed off down the hill. Is he going to be in trouble?"

King and Clarke looked at each other.

"We'll see," King said, feeling deflated. He had wanted it to be Norma Kincaid.

Norma folded her arms over her chest and then she dropped them, as the haughtiness seemed as if it melted from her face. "I am sorry, Kingsley Hartley."

"Huh?" King had turned toward the vehicle.

"I said," Norma swallowed, "I am sorry for saying that you would not amount to much, thirty years ago. I know that it still hurts you and I am genuinely sorry for saying it."

King couldn't believe what he was hearing.

Norma looked at Owen and then swallowed. "I liked you, you know. I had a crush on you back then and I said the worst things to you. I don't know why, who knows why they say the things they say sometimes. I didn't mean it and I regretted it the moment I said it. I realized what a blow it was to you."

King didn't know what to do. He was standing there like a statue.

"And," Norma sighed, "I guess you will hear this eventually but I am not a human trafficker. I was helping the anti-human trafficking task force with getting the people from this end of the food chain. Several persons in my field have been working with them."

"Oh." King felt foolish. Severely foolish.

"Don't feel bad about this," Norma sighed, "it is not advertised for a reason. If everybody knew we wouldn't be able to catch the bad guys. I was hoping that Regina would have dropped the whole thing and just shut up about her theories. I am sorry for the loss of your friend."

"Thank you," King said, his voice getting husky.

She nodded and watched him as he got into the car with Clarke.

"So where to now?" Clarke asked him jovially.

"The Cokes' Farm." King started the car. "What's it called again?"

"Rose Hill Farms," Clarke said, "That's where my wife buys our vegetables."

Chapter Twenty-One

Ruel drove up to Rose Hill farms. His hand was sweaty on the steering wheel and his heart was pounding like a jungle drum. When he had seen the name Coke in Jorja's diary he had blinked twice before it had sunk in what he was reading.

At first he thought it was her poor penmanship that was responsible for his misreading but he had quickly realized that Jorja's penmanship, though atrocious, made it plain for him to see who had gotten her pregnant.

To think a man could be so deceitful. He had looked him in the eye and hadn't even shown any indication of what he was up to...

It was similar to what he, Ruel, had done to Ashley...

He calmed down when he thought of that. It was very easy to condemn, wasn't it? And surely Jorja deserved her share of the blame, except he couldn't blame her for anything today because he had just confessed that she was laboring under the false assumption that her mother was dead.

He couldn't very well give her the lecture that she so well and truly deserved for lying to him, for pulling several people's names through the mud even though she knew she had never slept with them.

He heaved a sigh and tears came to his eyes. He must have some deceit gene. His daughter had inherited it. He got out of the car, feeling every inch of his forty years. If he had life to live over again, the first thing he would do was not marry Rosalie. He would search for Ashley after school and he would marry her instead.

But they hadn't been the same people, had they?

Ashley by her admission had not been the best of persons to know and maybe he had needed Rosalie's unsettling presence in his life to teach him patience. Maybe everything was the way it should be. He was sure that he was going to be a better person after this.

He got out of the car and slammed the door, and a navy blue car screeched to a halt beside him.

A fat short guy dressed in semi-formal wear got out and nodded to him.

He nodded back and then another guy got out. "Pastor Dennison."

"Yes." Ruel stiffened his spine.

"I am King." The man came around his side of the car and held out his hand.

Ruel shook it. "You are the detective that spoke to my wife yesterday?"

"Yes." King nodded.

"You are the detective that told Regina that I killed my wife?"

"I speculated," King said uncomfortably. "Did you?"

"No." Ruel grimaced. "She is still alive. So there goes that theory."

The short guy beside King cleared his throat.

"Oh right." King looked relieved to be stepping away from him.

"Well, er...sorry for the misunderstanding."

Ruel didn't reply. He walked behind them as they headed toward the offices. He wondered why they were there.

Charlotte was back and on the phone when they all walked in, but Ruel didn't pause to ask her any questions. He knew where to find Josiah's office. He had been there so many times before.

When he reached the door, it was wide-open, music blaring from his computer as he sat back and threw a ball and caught it as he talked on the phone.

"You," Ruel growled. His anger was back. "You slept with my daughter."

Josiah gasped and straightened up his office chair.

"I'll call you back," he murmured in the phone. "Pastor Ruel," he looked at the angry pastor and tried to calm him down, "that is quite a charge you have levied at me."

"How is the charge for murder, though?" King asked Josiah softly. "That one is infinitely worse."

*****

They had Josiah Coke cornered. The guilt was practically rolling off him. King grinned in satisfaction. Usually in a situation like this, he needed to know How? When? Why?

He already knew the how: Josiah gave her something she was allergic to and watched as she struggled to breathe. When? Sometime in the morning hours. Why? He thought he knew that too but as his assumptions were turning out to be less than accurate, he asked the question anyway. He was really interested in the answer.

"Why?" He didn't raise his voice. Josiah had turned down the music when they came to his office so he didn't need to speak loudly, but Josiah flinched as if whipped.

"What is going on here?" Conroy came to the office door and saw the three men in his son's office.

The pastor was the first to speak. "Conroy, it seems as if, er..." He looked at King, the shock still in his face, "that Josiah here is the, er, father of my daughter's unborn child and, er..."

"He killed Regina," King said. He didn't have any time for diplomacy and niceties. "And I just asked him why."

Conroy leaned on the doorjamb limply. "Josiah, you don't have to answer anything."

Josiah sighed and sank down in his chair. "Maybe I do."

He coughed and then looked down at his hands as if they were strange to him and he didn't know how they got there. The office was so quiet that they could hear Clarke's belly growl in the silence.

"I, er, I..." Josiah looked up. "When I was at Prism I siphoned off eighty million dollars from several accounts that I was working on over a two-year period. It was easy to get access to the high profile accounts because I was sleeping with my boss. I rationalized it by saying I used her; she used me."

Conroy gasped.

"When I told her that it was over, she started checking my work carefully and then she discovered what I had done. The company kept it quiet when they found out about it. It would have been bad for business if people knew that there was a problem with their accounts. They offered me a deal, pay back the money and they wouldn't press charges. I paid back the money; I had it in an account sitting down anyway, so it was no biggie to pay it back.

"When Regina came up here and I heard that she had background information on everyone, I figured that she probably knew something about me too. I visited her the same morning, after her big reveal. She was searching her suitcase frantically, trying to find her camera. She was mumbling that Lyn must have taken it and some files she had too. I asked her if she meant it about getting the police involved with everyone and she said yes. I asked her if she knew about my background and she laughed and said yes. Then she made a quip. 'Isn't it ironic that you are the church treasurer when you are a thief?'

"I told her that I didn't steal anymore and what I had done at Prism was not really stealing anyway. I did it to get back at my boss, to regain some power. Besides, I had given back the money.

"She said, 'You have nothing to worry about, Josiah, I was really after Norma Kincaid. She needs to be punished for her human trafficking, and Ruel Dennison, of course, he needs to go to prison for murdering his wife.'

"I told her that I was going back to church. She asked me if I wanted a drink. She took out a small flask of vodka and laughed when I grimaced. 'Live a little,' she said. 'After all, you already stole money, what's a little alcohol going to do?'

"I shook my head and told her bye. She said that since I was such a baby, maybe I should drink milk; Lyn Skinner kept peanut milk in the cupboard. I should get that and have a drink. Maybe if I stayed and talked to her I could save the whole lot of them from going to jail.

"So I got the milk. It was one of those small boxes that had a happy peanut on the side. I grabbed a glass, put some ice in the glass and came back in the room and sat across from Regina. I asked her if she was okay.

"She said she was sad, that Ashley was such a wimp and

didn't love her anymore. She said that she was twice the man that Ruel would ever be. I poured out the milk and was cradling my glass for a while, watching the ice melt, listening to her as she moaned about Ashley.

"I put my glass down on the table. I didn't know how to respond to her, so I leaned back in the settee and was preparing to listen for a while. Suddenly, in the midst of her conversation, she just reached for the glass and poured her vodka in it and chugged it down.

"Then she laughed a sad little laugh and looked at me, a smile on her face. 'That will teach her,' she said.

"I assumed the 'her' in this case was Ashley Dennison.

"I know she had allergies." Josiah shrugged. "Everybody did; Honey Allen has been telling the story all month how God struck Evil Regina with allergies. I had no idea that she was allergic to peanuts and milk.

"She laid down on the settee and told me that she needed to rest before she went to Kingston. She closed her eyes and said I should close the door on my way out.

"I did as she said. In the evening I was walking by and saw that her car was still in the garage so I decided to check if she was still around. I saw her in the settee still sleeping. So I left."

"Likely story," King snorted.

"But it is true." Josiah shrugged. "I am a lover not a fighter... well, killer."

Ruel winced.

"Besides, I had no motive for killing Regina," Josiah hurriedly added. "None. If she outed my past, the most that could happen was that I lose my treasurer post at church. I gave back the money I took from Prism and there are no criminal charges pending against me. I wouldn't be affected by any police investigation. I was just as shocked as anybody to hear that she died."

King growled. "Don't for one minute think that this is over. I will be watching you."

Josiah nodded. "Watch on."

*****

"His story lined up with the autopsy report," Detective Clarke said when they were outside. "Peanut milk and vodka. We found the vodka bottle in the crevice of the settee. She never accused Josiah of anything. He was always exempt. He had no motive to kill her."

When King reached the car he was breathing hard. He could hear his own breath in his ear.

"It was always a long shot," Clarke said soothingly. "There was no break-in, the locks on her bag weren't tampered with... the autopsy report said it was anaphylaxis...the people on her list to expose had nothing to fear from a police investigation. They had no motive. She did this herself, King. She knew she was allergic and she sent him for the drink and then she had it. Maybe she wanted somebody to be blamed for her demise. Who knows? "

"I had a hand in this." King's voice was broken. "I..."

"No blame," Clarke said genially. "Let it go. This was never a suspicious death case. I am going to the station to write my report; I have to concur with the coroner. There is nothing to see here."

*****

"You slept with my daughter, Josiah!" Ruel said through gritted teeth. "How could you sit there and watch while everybody including your own father was blamed for this pregnancy?"

Josiah hung his head. "She told me she had a crush on me and she started coming on to me at the office. Are you sure that I am the only person she slept with?"

Ruel gritted his teeth. "She is sure that you are. She was trying to protect you. She seems to think that she is in love."

Josiah sighed. "Okay."

"No, oh no!" Ruel growled. "It is not going to be that easy."

"I am not marrying her!" Josiah protested. "I don't care who she is."

"Who said anything about marriage?" Ruel growled. "All I want you to do is to announce to the church what you have done. That way you can clear Conroy and Owen's names. I have to say, Josiah, I expected better from you, I really did."

Conroy was still standing at the doorway. His face was frozen.

"Stealing...fornicating. I won't tell you what I am thinking right now, Josiah Coke. Maybe after Ruel leaves."

Chapter Twenty-Two

Ashley pulled the last suitcase to the veranda and looked at them. She remembered the very day that she moved in. She had been so happy and so relieved that the place was already furnished.

And she had been so in love and settled. Finally, she had thought, a woman like her, mistake-riddled and tainted by all of the stuff she had done, had scored a happy ending with a man of God—a Christian, a guy who could help her to stay in line.

She had been giddy with happiness then, but she didn't deserve a happy ending.

She had expected this, to be honest. She had been waiting for it…disappointment, tasting a bit of what she had dished out to Brandon.

She turned back to the house to see Jorja standing at the door, her eyes red and swollen. She looked as if she had just tumbled out of bed.

"What are you doing?" Jorja asked hoarsely.

"Leaving," Ashley said. "How are you holding up?"

"I'll live." Jorja sniffed. "I don't think you should leave. You really make Dad happy."

"How can you say that?" Ashley asked. "He lied to you, he lied to me, he lied to everybody."

"And you've never done that?" Jorja asked skeptically. "Lie to anyone, I mean...because I sure have."

Ashley shook her head. "That's beside the point. He told you your mother was dead. She's in a mental hospital somewhere and still alive.

"My mother is disturbed." Jorja shrugged, "I've always known that. I also know that eventually I wouldn't be able to live with her. I didn't say I am not disappointed in my father and his lies. I am disappointed. As I am sure he is disappointed in me. Can't you forgive him? Start afresh?"

"I don't know." Ashley shrugged. "It's just so...familiar, disturbingly familiar."

She had been here before but on the other side of the equation. She had been the one doing the lying and she remembered how desperately unhappy she was when everybody found out. She had made an ass of herself at Brandon's send-away party. She had pushed him too far.

That night she had gone home and cried, burdened and sorry, but unable to do anything about it because she had blown her chances.

"Where is Ruel?" Ashley asked.

"Gone to confront Josiah about my pregnancy."

Ashley opened her eyes wide. "But that means..."

"Yes," Jorja twisted her lips. "Yes, you guessed it, he's the one and the only ever possible candidate.

"Dad said that before he got kicked out of the church as pastor he was going to have a public confessional session and I am going to have to apologize to Uncle Owen and Uncle Conroy."

Ashley nodded, fair enough. "You did cause quite a stir with your accusations."

Jorja sighed. "I didn't want to implicate Josiah. I really like him but I don't think he likes me. I don't know...Uncle Owen was so easy to choose; he is so friendly...and Uncle Conroy—he was pining over Oliver's mom and didn't even realize that I was flirting with him."

"You have a lot of growing up to do, Jorja."

"I know." Jorja bit her lip. "Deal kindly with Dad, please."

She backed into the house and headed to her room. Ashley heard the door close softly; she sank down in a veranda chair.

Forgive us our trespasses as we forgive those who have trespassed against us. She repeated it over and over until she was dizzy with it.

"Sis Ashley." She opened her eyes slowly to see that Oliver was at the gate. He held up a large pot with the daffodils she had asked him about. It seemed like a lifetime ago now.

"Here they are."

"Ah." Ashley got up and headed for him. The bright yellow petals made her smile. "These are lovely, Oliver." She opened the gate. "Thank you."

Oliver smiled at her. "Did you know that daffodils represent forgiveness and new beginnings? In colder climates they signify the end of winter. They are like the symbolism of rebirth and renewal. It means winter is gone."

He placed them on the step. "It is raining again, so you shouldn't have any problems planting them out." He looked over at her bags in an ominous pile on the veranda and then over at her. "Or you can take them with you wherever you are going?"

"I am not sure if I am leaving for good," Ashley said,

realizing that to be true. "I might just stick around for a while if Ruel is here."

"Oh," Oliver nodded. "My mom is packing as well. She accepted a job offer in the Middle East. She said the pay is out of this world."

Ashley nodded. "And what about you?"

"Me." Oliver sighed, "I'll be staying with a distant relative in Kingston for my final year at high school, and then I am going to find my father."

"Oh." Ashley raised an eyebrow. "You know who he is?"

"No." Oliver shrugged. "I just know his name is Paul Scarlett from Treasure Beach. It should be quite easy to find his family and then after I find them, I should be able to find him." He shrugged. "Well, at least that's the plan."

Ashley smiled. "I hope you find them, Oliver, and I wish that all your dreams come true."

Ashley was still smiling when Oliver left.

She sat down on the veranda and admired her pot of daffodils. Forgiveness and new beginnings. She could do that. The old Ashley couldn't do that but maybe the new Ashley could.

Ruel came home just when she was putting back her last suitcase.

"Ash," his voice was husky, "can I dare to hope?"

"Oh yes," Ashley said, winking at him, "but first I am going to go back to Kingston, you are going to court me and then ask for my hand in marriage, and then we'll begin again, two flawed persons trying to live Godly lives."

Ruel nodded eagerly. "I can do that. Can it be fast-tracked? Say like a week."

Ashley grinned. "We'll see Ruel Dennison. We'll see."

Epilogue

Dear Sister Ashley,

It was good to see you and Pastor Ruel again after so many years. Thank you for coming to my graduation. And thank you for that bunch of daffodils; I can't believe that they are still around! I haven't seen daffodils in years.

We didn't get the chance to catch up, but I really wanted to find out about the folks back in Primrose Hill. Unfortunately, I lost touch with everyone there. I will be doing my internship at the university hospital and then I will be doing two years of medical missionary work in Africa—that is, according to my mom's plans. After that, I am free to live my life however I want to. :)

I found my father's family. They are good people. I have a lot of cousins and I hear that I have other brothers and a sister. My grandfather, Dolby Scarlett, was a fisherman, but he is long retired now. He is very interested in finding the missing Scarletts, as we've taken to calling them. When he met me he cried. I love that old man so much and wish that I had known him earlier.

Please don't stop writing and please update me; it was really good to see you again.

Your brother in Christ,
Oliver

Dear Oliver,

It was a pleasure to see your mail in my inbox this morning. We saw your mother in New York while on vacation on New Year's Eve and she made us promise to attend your graduation in the summer. It was our pleasure to come to your graduation. My, you have grown into a fine young man. If my daughter Alisha was in Jamaica I would definitely introduce you two but alas, she is at university in Canada.

We live in Montego Bay now; Ruel and I operate a guesthouse and wedding business. We are a one-stop wedding shop. From dresses to cakes, and everything you can think of, and we do have a gorgeous view. So remember us when you are ready to tie the knot. The offspring of the daffodils you gave me line the driveway of the guest-house. The place is called Daffodil House. You know, I still remember what you said about them being a symbol of new beginnings and renewal.

We go back to Primrose Hill quite often. Nothing much has changed. Sister Norma is still the queen bee. Bro. Owen is still the affable giant. He had a nasty bout of flu the other day and was admitted in the hospital, but he is out now, thank God. Jack is still Jack. He doesn't say much or do much.

Conroy got married a couple years ago to a widow; she had a daughter for him. I am sure your mother must have told you that. She talked my ear off, whining for the whole New Year's Eve about how Conroy is flaunting his happiness to her on Facebook.

Josiah and Jorja got married before she began to show. Ruel and Conroy twisted his arm about it.

You wouldn't be able to tell that the two of them were forced into marriage. They are quite happy together, surprisingly. They have two children now...

Am I leaving out anyone?

Oh yes, Nolan Ramsey. He is quite the popular televangelist these days. I am sure you have heard about him or seen him on local television. The other day I heard him telling our Primrose Hill story as part of a sermon. He called it 'Be careful how you perceive others and judge, everything may not be as it seems.' Very appropriate title from our Primrose Hill days.

I am happy you found your family, the Scarletts. I do hope you'll find your father, as well.

Thank you for writing, Oliver. May God continue to pour out his blessings on you. Continue to excel and to make a difference in this world.

Ashley

Author's Notes

Dear Reader,

THANK YOU for reading On The Rebound 2! I really wanted to bring a closure to Ashley's story and what happened in her life after Brandon ended their relationship. The character Oliver will appear again in the Scarlett Series, in fact he gets his own story. Look out for him in SCARLETT BRIDE.

The Scarlett Series is coming with another family who is filled with drama, romance, suspense and all of that mixed in. You can check my BOOK LIST, for the titles and release dates. In the meantime, turn the page for an excerpt from the first book in the Scarlett Series- SCARLETT BABY.

You can be among the first to hear when I have special prices and new book releases by signing up for my mailing list. It will take you less than 50 seconds to signup. Signup for my mailing list at brenda-barrett.com

Thanks again. All the best,

Brenda

**Here is the first chapter of
SCARLETT BABY**

Good friend, why did you have to go... The Kenny Rogers song that belted across the expanse of the yard held his heart tightly and squeezed.

Yuri sat heavily in one of the white plastic chairs that his mother had thoughtfully placed around the yard. His eyes were stinging and he swiped his hand over them impatiently. He was bone tired. It was a long journey from Kingston and his tedious middle management job. He had a headache, heartache, a toothache, all of him ached... Excuses.

He held his head down. He was determined not to let the tears fall. He was sure if he tried to think about something else the song would release its hold on him but it kept pulsing through his head.

He breathed a sigh of relief and inhaled a refreshing gulp of air when the verse faded away...and in my memories you'll always be a good, good friend to me... He had barely, just barely saved himself from an embarrassing crying jag.

He was relieved when his cousin, who seemed to be standing in as the deejay, put in a Temptations album and left it to play. But even that was nostalgic, especially when he heard the first notes from Soul to Soul. If he was being so tearful now, he wondered how he was going to hold up tomorrow at the burial.

Burial. He hated the word. And he hated it even more when it was attached to his grandfather. Dolby Scarlett had always been more than family. He had been a really good friend to him. They had shared countless memories and numerous confidences, but now he was gone. Though why he should feel the grief so sharply he didn't know. His grandfather had a good inning, one hundred years old. A solid century.

Maybe he was feeling so ripped up inside because he had not been able to get time off from his job to come home and see Pops one last time. Six months ago when he had returned home, he had poured out all of his confused feelings and maddening failings to Pops and his grandfather had confidently told him that it would all work out. He wished that he had had a more upbeat conversation with Pops that last time.

"Want a drink, honey?" his mother asked, looking at him sympathetically. "You haven't had anything to eat or drink since you arrived."

"No thanks, Mom." His voice was low and choked up. "When I'm ready I'll come and get it and maybe socialize then."

His mother patted his hand and moved away, too busy with the scores of people who were trailing into the yard to question him further.

He watched the buzzing activity but felt detached from it. In this community a death in the family warranted some amount of preparation. And Pops was so well known that on the eve of the big sendoff it was almost like a party. His parents had set up a shed where people were cooking; he recognized that Fred was leading the procedures there. He was the official dead yard cook. He was stirring a pot almost as tall as he was; the scent of the goat head soup wafted to where he was sitting.

He spotted family members he hadn't seen in ages. They were gathering around in clusters. He overheard conversations about grave digging and which suit they would put Pops in for the viewing. Yuri avoided eye contact with anyone who would want to involve him in their decisions.

He answered greetings in a desultory manner, even had a

conversation with a family friend or two, and watched as the late June sun bathed the spacious yard in a mellow yellowed hue. It was, ironically, the perfect evening to be in Treasure Beach. It was not too hot yet, nor was it cool—June had just begun. It was just right. The skies were endlessly blue, with not a cloud in sight.

His family had always lived in this spot in Great Bay. The half-acre of shrub land was located a few feet from the sea. It was rocky in some places, fertile in others.

Through the years they had wrangled with the stony soil and deleterious effects of the wind and had managed to get a few trees growing.

He was sitting under one now, a red plum tree. Its gnarled limbs were devoid of leaves. It was that time of the year when it would shed; in a few weeks it would be loaded with leaves, and then the juicy red plums would take over the tree. His grandfather had loved to munch on them.

He closed his eyes and leaned back in the chair. He heard the gentle lapping of the sea a few yards from where he was sitting, the buzz of chatter near the house, a dog barking, somebody coughing, his father's voice and then his sister's finer, sweeter tones responding to something that his father said, and then the lump of grief that was stuck in his throat subsided.

He felt a shadow before him and he opened his eyes slowly.

Terri was standing before him. She had a drink in her hand, she pushed it at him.

"Drink."

"What is it?" Yuri asked, his voice husky.

"Fruit juice. Daddy blended it for you."

"Ah." Yuri took a sip and then drained the cup's contents into his mouth. It was good. His father always did a mean fruit juice.

Terri pulled a chair and sat beside him. "You left your bag on the veranda; that's how I knew you were here."

"Sorry." Yuri sighed. "I couldn't go into the house. I felt a bit..."

"Overwhelmed," Terri finished for him, "crazy with grief. I understand. Though I am sure with how tight you and Pops were, this must be worse for you than anyone else, even Daddy."

Yuri nodded. He didn't have to respond. He glanced at his sister; the sun bathed her in a golden glow. He realized that he hadn't seen Terri for months now, and he hadn't even greeted her properly.

"Hey," he smiled at her.

Terri smiled back; she was a strikingly good-looking woman. She had dark brown skin, clay red hair and light hazel eyes.

Grandfather's eyes.

The only one in the family to get them as far as he knew. One could never tell how many Scarletts there were because of Peter Scarlett, his grandfather's youngest child. It was said that Peter sired quite a few children. It was just last year that he met his cousin, Oliver.

And Grandfather's hair. The red-brown combination was prominent with Pop's brothers and sisters and their offspring. His little niece Dahlia had gotten it too.

"How long have you been here?"

"I came in last night." Terri sighed, "I am flying out tomorrow after the funeral."

"That sucks," Yuri murmured.

"No, it's fine. At least I got the time off." Terri grimaced, "I am sort of getting weary of the job."

"You were so excited when you started last year." Yuri grinned. "You were going places, France, Switzerland and all over. What changed?"

"The thrill wore off." Terri shrugged. "Enough about me, tell me about you. You look as if you aren't sleeping much."

"True." Yuri nodded. "I know I look like hell."

"No, never. Stop fishing for compliments, Big Head." Terri elbowed him. "You have always been seriously good-looking and even though you are my brother I can see that you have a little Shemar Moore thing going on."

Yuri chuckled. "Well, thanks."

"So answer. Why are you looking like lukewarm porridge?" Terri asked. "Apart from the fact that we are here for the funeral and the fact that you always look gutted when you come back here, whether it's a funeral or a wedding. Remember Troy's wedding? You sat in a corner and you looked whipped, like some evil pixie had given you a beating."

He remembered Troy's wedding. His little brother had gotten married five years ago, two days before Marla and Ricky's wedding. Of course he had been gutted. He had been best man at both affairs and he had thought that he had hid his displeasure quite well.

But of course, Terri had made it her personal job to psychoanalyze him and probe into his mind and had seen how devastated he had been at the time, even though he thought he had acted pretty well, considering.

"Is there a point to this?" Yuri looked at his sister in disgust.

Terri's eyes brightened considerably when she saw his expression. "Much better--you look less woebegone when you have that battle light in your eyes."

Yuri kissed his teeth. "Whatever."

"So why are you so sad looking?" Terri prompted.

Yuri gave her an assessing look. "This is strictly between us. You can't tell Mom and Dad, or Troy."

"As if," Terri snorted. "When have I ever let out a confidence?"

"You told everyone that I liked Marla."

"For goodness' sakes, Yuri. You were fifteen. I was ten. Besides, the whole family knew, the neighborhood knew. I am pretty sure that one look at you and everybody in the world would have known! That was thirteen years ago." Terri looked at him slyly. "You still like her, don't you...after all these years?"

"No!" Yuri protested quickly. "No, of course not; she's married to my best friend."

"Ricardo Mills is not worthy to be called your friend." Terri snorted. "Why you still have him in your life is beyond me."

"He likes to keep in touch," Yuri murmured, "so we keep in touch."

"He likes to torture you and let you know that he won... that he got the girl," Terri said harshly. "I am absolutely not sorry that he had that accident and was paralyzed...that should keep the loud mouthed-bully humble."

"Terri!" Yuri looked at her sharply. "I was responsible for that accident!"

"No, you weren't. He wants you to think so," Terri said stubbornly. "You know what, enough of this. You were going to tell me something before we went down this road."

"I don't feel like telling you anything anymore," Yuri grumbled.

"You'd better," Terri pinched him, "or else I am going to gently suggest to Mommy that you look like hell and it's not because you are grieving. Then Mommy will hound you and call you all hours of the day and night, finding out if you have eaten and if you have brushed your teeth, if you are overworking and..."

"Okay, threat received and processed." Yuri grinned. "She

stopped doing that to you yet?"

"Nope." Terri smiled. "It has gotten a little better, though. I think I have passed the adult test because I am a flight attendant now."

Yuri looked up at the tree limbs and then at Terri. "The company where I work is selling out. Three of the guys are planning to buy it from the owner. They asked me if I wanted in. It is a good deal. They sell electronic circuit boards and the software division that I manage is on the cusp of a few break-throughs. So this would be a good...no, not just good... an excellent deal."

"So what's wrong?" Terri asked innocently, as if she had forgotten that the Scarletts were not exactly the richest people in the world.

Yuri laughed. "Terri, I can barely afford my rent and I am still paying back student loans. Where would I find millions of dollars to buy into this venture? Unlike the other guys I am not from a wealthy background."

Terri nodded. "I see."

"It has been keeping me up at nights." Yuri clenched and unclenched his fingers. "I talked to Grandpa about it couple months ago too..."

"Really?" Terri said, "Why am I not surprised? You tell him everything."

"I got a bit desperate and talked to Ricky about it too."

"Why?" Terri's voice got frosty. "Of all the people in the world…really?"

"He's rich," Yuri said simply, "and he is my friend. You keep forgetting that."

"He wouldn't lift a finger if you were in trouble." Terri pointed out. "He is a phony who for some strange reason wants everything you have or want, which is very puzzling to me since he is the one that was born with a silver spoon in his mouth."

Yuri sighed. "He said he would help."

"A deal with the devil," Terri snorted. "What does he want in return, service from your unborn children, a right hand and a foot, no...wait, bet he wants you to paralyze yourself too, so that the two of you can be equals."

"He wants a baby." Yuri sighed. "Well, Marla wants a baby. And instead of some strange sperm donor and all the works, they want my sperm. Someone they know and trust."

There was silence after his statement.

Terri looked like she was finding it hard to process what he said.

"Terri," Yuri prompted in the silence.

"Don't." Terri swallowed, her face serious and tense. "Do not do it; let Ricky find some other sucker to give him a baby."

"I didn't say I would," Yuri rebuked her gently. "It wouldn't be right."

"He is just looking for a way to torture you because you are no longer under his spell. You escaped the country and seeing him and Marla together, you are now living in Kingston far away from him and he doesn't know what you are doing. So he has to find some way of hanging on to you from afar.

"He is so obsessed with controlling you that he wants a child by you and the woman that you love to make him feel better about himself." Terri was roiled up. "Poor little rich boy Ricky Mills has all the wealth in the world but he can't be Yuri Scarlett. He's obsessed!"

Yuri had never seen Ricky the way that Terri did and he was quite taken aback by Terri's assessment of the situation. But despite her disdain for Ricky he was still tempted to do it. How else could he come up with thirty million dollars? He didn't know anybody else who would be willing to give him that amount of money or even hear the figure and not gasp in astonishment.

Ricky had just calmly asked him when he wanted the money. Just like that. No fanfare, no questions; he hadn't even explained what the company was about or his plan to pay him back.

Was it really a deal with the devil, as Terri had so dramatically put it? He wished he had his grandfather to discuss this with. He hadn't gotten the chance to in the last couple of weeks when Pops got sick; it wouldn't have been fair to burden him with his problems.

He couldn't tell his parents. His mother was a worrier, and this sort of problem would be beyond their comprehension. They were poor country folks; telling them that he needed thirty million dollars was like speaking another language.

His father was a farmer and his mother a housewife and it was only just last year that they had even finished the house. The four-bedroom structure had stood half finished for years, a sore in the eyes of the community, but his parents had not been able to afford fixing it up. They had sacrificed and sent all three of their children through college. Education before aesthetics was his mother's constant mantra.

"Here comes company," Terri whispered, breaking into his reverie.

Yuri looked across the yard, all the way to the front, and his heart skipped a beat. Marla was parking her BMW beside his battered Ford Escort.

"It took her long enough to show up," Terri murmured. "Maybe she just heard that you arrived, or maybe evil Ricky has finally let her out of the house. You know, it wouldn't surprise me if he told her not to fraternize with us common folks."

Yuri didn't respond. He had long hardened his heart against

having feelings for Marla. He had long mastered the art of only showing her a friendly face.

But now, just now, when she climbed out of the car in her khaki shorts and her white vest top, showing off her honey-gold skin, he had a lapse.

A brief lapse.

He was thinking of her carrying his baby and he had to admit to himself that this was not the first time he had done so. This very thought was what was keeping him up at nights...

an adult learning class. Only to find out that his crush was his teacher. Surely a woman like her would not be interested in an uneducated man from the slums?

Scarlett Promise (Book 5)- After overhearing a whispered conversation that revealed her true parentage, Lisa Barclay ran away from home. She quickly found out that surviving on the gritty streets of Kingston was an uphill battle. Driven by desperation she decides to make some extra money by prostituting herself. Her first customer turns out to be a popular government senator and then to her horror he dies...

Scarlett Bride (Book 6)- Oliver Scarlett loved his job as a missionary doctor in the rarely visited, highly populated village of Kidogo, located in the midlands of the Congo region. He rescued a young village woman from a horrible fate of marrying the old witch doctor by marrying her himself. Now it is time to return home, he has to take his newly acquired bride with him or rescuing her would have been in vain.

Scarlett Heart (Book 7)- After receiving a heart transplant shy librarian Noah Scarlett started to take on character traits that were unlike him. He was going to the gym and loving cherry malt sodas and he kept dreaming of a girl named Charlotte Green...

Rebound Series

On The Rebound - For Better or Worse, Brandon vowed to stay with Ashley, but when worse got too much he moved out and met Nadine. For the first time in years he felt happy, but then Ashley remembered her wedding vows...

On The Rebound 2- Ashley reinvented herself and was now a first lady in a country church in Primrose Hill, but her obsessed ex friend Regina showed up and started digging into the lives of the saints at church. Somebody didn't like Regina's digging. Someone had secrets that were shocking enough to kill for...

Magnolia Sisters

Dear Mystery Guy (Book 1) - Della Gold details her life in a journal dedicated to a mystery guy. But when fascination turns into obsession she finds herself wanting to learn even more about him but in her pursuit of the mystery guy she begins to learn more about herself...

Bad Girl Blues (Book 2) - Brigid Manderson wanted to go to med school but for the time being she was an escort working for her mother, an ex-prostitute. When her latest customer offers her the opportunity of a lifetime would she take it? Or would she choose the harder path and uncertain love with a Christian guy?

Her Mistaken Dreams (Book 3) - Caitlin Denvers dream guy had serious issues. He has a dead wife in his past and he was the main suspect in her murder. Did he really do it? Or did Caitlin for the first time have a mistaken dream?

Just Like Yesterday (Book 4) - Hazel Brown lost six months of memory including the summer that she conceived her son, and had no idea who his father could be. Now that she had the means to fight to get him back from the Deckers, she finds out that the handsome Curtis Decker is willing to share her son with her after all.

New Song Series

Going Solo (Book 1) - Carson Bell, had a lovely voice, a heart of gold, and was no slouch in the looks department. So why did Alice abandon him and their daughter? What did she want after ten years of silence?

Duet on Fire (Book 2) - Ian and Ruby had problems trying to conceive a child. If that wasn't enough, her ex-lover the current pastor of their church wants her back...

Tangled Chords (Book 3) - Xavier Bell, the poor, ugly duckling has made it rich and his looks have been incredibly improved too. Farrah Knight, hotel heiress had cruelly rejected him in the past but now she needed help. Could Xavier forgive and forget?

Broken Harmony(Book 4) - Aaron Lee, wanted the top job in his family company but he had a moral clause to consider just when Alka, his married ex-girlfriend walks back into his life.

A Past Refrain (Book 5) - Jayce had issues with forgetting Haley Greenwald even though he had a new woman in his life. Will he ever be able to shake his love for Haley?

Perfect Melody (Book 6) - Logan Moore had the perfect wife, Melody but his secretary Sabrina was hell bent on breaking up the family. Sabrina wanted Logan whatever the cost and she had a secret about Melody, that could shatter Melody's image to everyone.

The Bancroft Family Series

Homely Girl (Book 0) - April and Taj were opposites in so many ways. He was the cute, athletic boy that everybody wanted to be friends with. She was the overweight, shy, and withdrawn girl. Do April and Taj have a love that can last a lifetime? Or will time and separate paths rip them apart?

Saving Face (Book 1) - Mount Faith University drama begins with a dead president and several suspects including the president in waiting Ryan Bancroft.

Tattered Tiara (Book 2) - Micah Bancroft is targeted by femme fatale Deidra Durkheim. There are also several rape cases to be solved.

Private Dancer (Book 3) - Adrian Bancroft was gutted when he returned to Jamaica and found out that his first and only love Cathy Taylor was a stripper and was literally owned by the menacing drug lord, Nanjo Jones.

Goodbye Lonely (Book 4) - Kylie Bancroft was shy and had to resort to going to confidence classes. How could she win the love of Gareth Beecher, her faculty adviser, a man with a jealous ex-wife in his past and a current mystery surrounding a hand found in his garden?

Practice Run (Book 5) - Marcus Bancroft had many reasons to avoid Mount Faith but Deidra Durkheim was not one of them. Unfortunately, on one of his visits he was the victim of a deliberate hit and run.

Sense of Rumor (Book 6) - Arnella Bancroft was the

wild, passionate Bancroft, the creative loner who didn't mind living dangerously; but when a terrible thing happened to her at her friend Tracy's party, it changed her. She found that courting rumors can be devastating and that only the truth could set her free.

A Younger Man (Book 7) - Pastor Vanley Bancroft loved Anita Parkinson despite their fifteen-year age gap, but Anita had a secret, one that she could not reveal to Vanley. To tell him would change his feelings toward her, or force him to give up the ministry that he loved so much.

Just To See Her (Book 8) - Jessica Bancroft had the opportunity to meet her fantasy guy Khaled, he was finally coming to Mount Faith but she had feelings for Clay Reid, a guy who had all the qualities she was looking for. Who would she choose and what about the weird fascination Khaled had for Clay?

The Three Rivers Series

Private Sins (Book 1) - Kelly, the first lady at Three Rivers Church was pregnant for the first elder of her church. Could she keep the secret from her husband and pretend that all was well?

Loving Mr. Wright (Book 2) - Erica saw one last opportunity to ditch her single life when Caleb Wright appeared in her town. He was perfect for her, but what was he hiding?

Unholy Matrimony (Book 3) - Phoebe had a problem, she was poor and unhappy. Her solution to marry a rich man was derailed along the way with her feelings for Charles Black, the poor guy next door.

If It Ain't Broke (Book 4) - Chris Donahue wanted a place in his child's life. Pinky Black just wanted his love. She also wanted him to forget his obsession with Kelly and love her. That shouldn't be so hard? Should it?

Contemporary Romance/Drama

After The End - Torn between two lovers. Colleen married her high school sweetheart, Isaiah, hoping that they would live happily ever after but life intruded and Isaiah disappeared at sea. She found work with the rich and handsome, Enrique Lopez, as a housekeeper and realized that she couldn't keep him at arms length...

Love Triangle: Three Sides To The Story - George, the husband, Marie, the wife and Karen-the mistress. They all get to tell their side of the story.

The Preacher And The Prostitute - Prostitution and the clergy don't mix. Tell that to ex-prostitute, Maribel, who finds herself in love with the Pastor at her church. Can an ex-prostitute and a pastor have a future together?

New Beginnings - Inner city girl Geneva was offered an opportunity of a lifetime when she found out that her 'real' father was a very wealthy man. Her decision to live uptown meant that she had to leave Froggie, her 'ghetto don,' behind. She also found herself battling with her stepmother and battling her emotions for Justin, a suave up-towner.

Full Circle - After graduating from university, Diana wanted to return to Jamaica to find her siblings. What she didn't foresee was that she would meet Robert Cassidy and that both their pasts would be intertwined, and that disturbing questions would pop up about their parentage, just when they were getting close.

Historical Fiction/Romance

The Empty Hammock - Workaholic, Ana Mendez, fell asleep in a hammock and woke up in the year 1494. It was the time of the Tainos, a time when life seemed simpler, but Ana knew that all of that was about to change.

The Pull Of Freedom - Even in bondage the people, freshly arrived from Africa, considered themselves free. Led by Nanny and Cudjoe the slaves escaped the Simmonds' plantation and went in different directions to forge their destiny in the new country called Jamaica.

Jamaican Comedy (Material contains Jamaican dialect)

Di Taxi Ride And Other Stories - Di Taxi Ride and Other Stories is a collection of twelve witty and fast paced short stories. Each story tells of a unique slice of Jamaican life.

CPSIA information can be obtained
at www.ICGtesting.com
Printed in the USA
LVOW13s1617231216
518585LV00009B/261/P